'You are a caring and competent surgeon who has a way with children and would make a wonderful mother.'

To be told that Aaron thought she would make a good mother brought the tears back again, and as they streamed down her cheeks his expression changed from incomprehension to awareness.

'That's it, isn't it?' he exclaimed. 'You want a child of your own. The ache inside you comes from that, and because you've been on your own for so long you can't cope with making that sort of commitment.'

'Yes, that's it,' she agreed, glad to be off the hook. If she had to lie, she had to lie, and at that moment the truth would have choked her in the telling.

Aaron was smiling. He couldn't help it. He'd solved the mystery. With patience and careful wooing it might all come right for them.

**Abigail Gordon** loves to write about the fascinating combination of medicine and romance from her home in a Cheshire village. She is active in local affairs and is even called upon to write the script for the annual village pantomime! Her eldest son is a hospital manager, and helps with all her medical research. As part of a close-knit family, she treasures having two of her sons living close by and the third one not too far away. This also gives her the added pleasure of being able to watch her delightful grandchildren growing up.

**Recent titles by the same author:**

THE POLICE SURGEON'S RESCUE
THE GP'S SECRET
IN-FLIGHT EMERGENCY
THE PREGNANT POLICE SURGEON

# THE SURGEON'S FAMILY WISH

BY
ABIGAIL GORDON

MILLS & BOON®

*All the characters in this book have no existence outside the imagination of the author, and have no relation whatsoever to anyone bearing the same name or names. They are not even distantly inspired by any individual known or unknown to the author, and all the incidents are pure invention.*

*First published in Great Britain 2004*
*Harlequin Mills & Boon Limited,*
*Eton House, 18-24 Paradise Road, Richmond, Surrey TW9 1SR*

© Abigail Gordon 2004

ISBN 0 263 83928 1

*Set in Times Roman 10½ on 12 pt.*
*03-1004-49104*

*Printed and bound in Spain*
*by Litografia Rosés, S.A., Barcelona*

# CHAPTER ONE

AARON LEWIS was smiling as it was announced that the aircraft was preparing for landing. The last two weeks spent touring foreign hospitals and noting different techniques had been absorbing, but here was where his heart was. In the English city where he worked in a large children's hospital and lived in a rambling, red-brick house with what was left of his family.

His smile deepened as he envisaged them waiting for him at the airport. His mother, her round pink face alight with pleasure at the sight of him, with Lucy beside her, dancing with excitement because he was back. They were his world and every time he saw a sick child he gave thanks for his daughter's good health.

Ever since the day when his wife had gone into the sea in a Cornish cove to go to the assistance of his father, who'd been caught in a fast and dangerous current, there'd been just the three of them—his mother, his daughter and himself.

He'd gone back to the hotel that day with Lucy, then a toddler, for something they'd forgotten, and by the time he'd got back to the beach his wife and father had both been swept out to sea.

There'd been a huge search, with the lifeboat and air-sea rescue services involved, but to no avail, and when their bodies had been washed up with the tide a couple of days later, both he and his mother had been faced with the knowledge that half of a close, loving family was gone.

5

Eloise had drowned trying to save her adored father-in-law and as Aaron had stood gazing bleakly out to sea on the golden sand where they'd been picnicking on that terrible day, his mother had said, 'Life has to go on, Aaron, for Lucy's sake if nothing else.'

That had been four years ago and they'd coped. As long as he didn't look back too much, life had been reasonably good. His mother had taken Eloise's place in Lucy's young life, while he'd done his best to take care of them both. In a very short time the threesome would be reunited.

As he waited for his luggage to come round on the carousel Aaron was imagining his daughter's face when she saw what he'd brought her back from the trip. He'd spoken to her every night while he'd been away but it hadn't been the same as holding Lucy in his arms.

Yet there was only his mother waiting to greet him when he'd gone through the formalities. No Lucy, and her grandmother's face was pinched and grey. He could smell trouble a mile off. It went with the job, and he'd only seen his mother look like this once before.

As Mary Lewis watched her son approach she knew she was about to blight his homecoming. He was a commanding figure, striding towards her amongst the other travellers. Tall, straight, with dark hair curling above his ears, his eyes were like soft brown velvet when they rested upon his family and his small patients. They could also be as hard as flint if he came across a situation that did not please him....

She saw his brisk stride falter and swallowed hard.

'What's wrong?' he asked the moment he reached her side. 'Where's Lucy?'

Her smooth cheeks were crumpling, but her voice was steady as she told him, 'She's in Barnaby's, Aaron. Lucy fell off the climbing frame in the garden yesterday and instead of landing on the grass cracked her head on the lawnmower that I'd left nearby while I went to answer the phone. She must have fallen awkwardly. By the time I got to her she was unconscious. I sent for an ambulance. They took us to the General and from there they transferred Lucy to Barnaby's.'

'Why?' he questioned tightly as his worst nightmare took on form and shape. 'Why did they transfer her? And why didn't you let me know?'

He'd taken hold of his mother's arm and was ushering her towards the exit, not wanting to waste a moment in getting to his daughter's side.

'They X-rayed her head in A and E and did a CT scan which revealed an open fracture of the skull requiring surgery. The new paediatric surgeon at Barnaby's took over from there. As to why I didn't let you know, I rang your hotel but you'd just left for the airport, and I decided that you would be better making the long flight without having a terrible anxiety gnawing at you.'

'How is Lucy now?' he asked in the same tight tone. 'Any brain damage?'

'You need to talk to the doctor who operated. I was so agitated I could hardly take in what she was saying. The main thing at the moment is that Lucy has come through it and was sleeping peacefully when I left her. I've been with her all the time, needless to say, but I had to come to meet you. I couldn't let you walk into something so worrying without warning.'

She was almost running to keep up with him and, contrite, he slowed down. Putting his arm around her shoulders, he gave her a quick hug.

'You are the best. You do know that, don't you?'

Her smile was wry. 'I didn't feel like that yesterday when I saw our little one lying so still.'

'No, I can imagine,' he said gently, adding, with the urgency in him unabated, 'Where have you parked the car?'

'Across the way there,' she told him, passing him the keys. 'You'd better drive, Aaron. We'll get there more quickly and I'm beginning to wilt now that I've passed the burden on to you.'

'I'm sorry that you've had to cope with this on your own, Mum,' he told her regretfully. 'It must have been horrendous, but we'll be with Lucy soon and then I'll be able to find out for myself what the damage is.'

He groaned.

'I can't believe that the moment I turn my back the fates start playing tricks. *My* daughter in *my* hospital. And you said it's someone new who operated on Lucy. Where was Charles, for heaven's sake, and Mark Lafferty?'

Charles Drury was the consultant, who was shortly to retire after a long career in paediatric surgery, and the other man was a skilled surgeon in his fifties. It was surprising that neither of them had been available to operate on his precious child.

'Charles is away on holiday,' his mother informed him, 'and Mark is incapacitated with a broken pelvis after a motor accident. It was a Dr Swain who operated on Lucy. It was her first day at Barnaby's and she looked washed out, as if she should be in bed herself.'

Aaron nodded grimly.

'Yes, of course. I'd forgotten. She would be the new broom. We've had a lot of staff changes recently on the surgical side. Thankfully my lot don't have such itchy feet.'

He was hoping that this new woman was up to scratch. Not all the surgeons who operated on the children that he and his staff had in their care were of Charles Drury's standard.

The hospital gates were looming up. He would soon know how well the Swain woman did her job.

He was almost galloping as they reached the main corridor of the hospital and his mother said, 'Go on, I'll catch you up. Lucy is in a small room off Rainbow Ward.'

In the early October morning the ward was beginning to come to life. Nurses flitted amongst the beds, talking gently to those who were fretful and with a cheerful word for the rest.

The sister saw him the moment he came whizzing in and she flashed him a sympathetic smile.

'Not a good day for you, is it, Dr Lewis, but Lucy is making good progress,' she said as he made towards the side ward. 'She came through the operation satisfactorily and is still sleeping. Dr Swain is on her way to see her.'

Aaron felt tears prick as he stood beside the still form of his daughter. She was so small to have to go through that kind of surgery, but there was a ward full of children out there and none of *their* problems were minor. Rainbow Ward was for the more serious cases and the Lollipop Ward for those less complicated, but often they overflowed into each other.

Lucy's fair curls had been shorn off and the part of her scalp where surgery had been performed was covered in dressings. She looked so little and vulnerable he could hardly bear it, but there were things he had to know. The extent of the damage to her skull. What amount of surgery had been necessary. And the best person to tell him that was Dr Swain.

The sister had left him to go back to supervising in the main ward, and as Aaron was lifting the clipboard from the bottom rail of the bed to read Lucy's notes the door opened.

She was tall, slender, with nut-brown shoulder-length hair framing a tired, white face. But tired or not, her glance, when it met his, was cool and professional and her grip firm as she introduced herself.

'I'm Annabel Swain,' she said quietly, 'and you must be Dr Lewis, Lucy's father.'

'Yes,' he told her, and without going into any of the niceties added, 'I need to know how badly hurt my daughter was and what surgery you've performed on her.'

'Yes, of course,' she agreed. Sinking down onto a chair beside the bed, she looked up at him.

There was weariness behind the cool hazel gaze meeting his, but it barely registered. Aaron was frantic to know the worst. Once he'd absorbed it he would cope. At least Lucy was alive and who knew better than he what terrible damage could be caused to children *and* adults in accidental happenings?

'Lucy was transferred to Barnaby's from A and E last night as I was about to finish my shift,' she told him in a voice that he would have thought pleasing to the ear at any other time. 'She was unconscious and had been diagnosed with an open skull fracture.

'Fortunately, I have done some specialising in neurology and problems of the cranium and operated immediately to correct fragmentation of the bone and prevent her condition worsening.'

'What about brain damage?' he asked quickly. 'Any penetration of the meninges and brain tissue?'

She shook her head and the brown hair swung gently around her pale face.

'None that I could see. I drained away surplus blood and repaired damaged vessels, along with realigning the fractured bone. I shall be keeping a close watch on Lucy for the next few days. She was unconscious before the operation but she's sleeping naturally now.' She was getting to her feet. 'But as Head of Paediatrics I'm sure you won't need me to tell you that.'

'You can tell me anything you like as long as it's beneficial to Lucy,' he told her, and sent up a prayer of thankfulness that this woman *had* known what she was doing.

'I'm living in hospital accommodation at the moment in a flat at the other side of the grounds,' she was explaining. 'I'm going there to get some sleep once I've made sure that your daughter is all right. If you need me for anything, don't hesitate to ring me. I've already told Sister to call me the moment she wakes up, but it could be some time before Lucy surfaces from the trauma of the operation and the effects of the anaesthetic. When she does, that will be crunch time.'

Aaron nodded.

'I realise that, and if you need sleep by all means go and get it. A tired doctor is not a good one. It would seem that you came to us at a bad time, with two of our paediatric surgeons not available.'

Her smile was wry.

'Yes...and *you* weren't around either.'

'No, I wasn't,' he agreed sombrely. 'I wish I had been.'

'But Lucy's grandma was there.'

'Yes,' he said levelly. 'My mother is always there

when we need her. Our three generations jog along together very well.'

As Annabel Swain threw herself down on top of sheets that hadn't been slept between for two days she was thinking about the man she'd just met. Since becoming involved with Lucy she had discovered that the absent head of Paediatrics at Barnaby's Children's Hospital was someone of note.

He was referred to with respect and deference and she'd wondered why. Now that she'd met him she understood in part. He had a commanding presence…and a very attractive one, too. She might be disenchanted with the opposite sex but a man like him was so easy on the eye she wasn't going to overlook that.

She'd sensed back there in the ward that he'd had his doubts about her, would have preferred his daughter to be operated on by one of the regular surgeons, but if that was the case it was too bad. Yet she couldn't blame him. It was clear to see that he was a loving father and it must have been horrendous to come home to find his daughter had been given emergency surgery in his absence by a stranger instead of a close colleague.

There didn't appear to be any mother in the family set-up, so he must be either divorced or a widower. Neither situation very unusual. Both the kind of set-up where a loving grandmother would be welcome.

His mother had arrived at the ward just as Annabel was leaving and the two women had spoken briefly.

'How is Lucy now?' Mary Lewis had asked anxiously when they'd come face to face, and Annabel had thought how lovely it would be to have a mother like this kindly, chubby woman.

She'd managed a tired smile. 'Progressing satisfactorily,' she'd told her. 'Pulse and temperature normal. No post-operative complications at the moment. But as her father is only too aware, there is still a possibility of brain damage.'

The colour had drained from the older woman's face.

'Oh, no!'

'I've told your son that there were no signs of damage to the brain or the meninges, but one can't be sure until the patient is fully awake and over the effects of the operation,' Annabel had told her. 'Now, if you'll excuse me, I'm going off duty for a while to get some sleep.'

The anxious grandmother had flashed her a sympathetic smile.

'Yes, of course, my dear. You must be exhausted. Thank you for taking such good care of our little one.'

'It's my job,' Annabel had told her, and as she'd walked through the hospital grounds to the utilitarian flat she was renting because she couldn't be bothered to start house-hunting, she'd thought that there hadn't been any thanks coming from Aaron Lewis. But she could forgive him for that. He would be on a knife edge until Lucy opened her eyes. Praying that he would see lucid normality there.

She'd been looking forward to being a parent herself not so long ago. But a fall on a wet tiled floor in a hospital corridor while moving at speed had sent her crashing down and had brought an end to all her hopes and dreams.

If it had been in the first weeks after she'd found out she was to have a child, Annabel might have felt she'd had a lucky escape after her affair with an American doctor had dwindled and died when she'd discovered he had a wife and family back in the States. But at four months into the pregnancy Annabel had settled into the role of prospective single parent and had been eagerly looking forward to the birth of her child. Now, bereft and lonely after her shamefaced lover had returned to his homeland, she was doing the job she'd always done, using her skills to try to save or improve the lives of other people's children, and all the time she was mourning the loss of her own baby.

As she lay looking up at the drab ceiling the memory of her affair with Randolph Graham was preventing sleep. They'd worked together in Paediatrics in a big Middlesex hospital where he'd come to do a twelve-month exchange and Annabel, in her thirties, having spent all her working life caring for the children of others, had been happy to discover her pregnancy with the amiable American as her partner.

But when he heard that the two of them had made a child, everything had changed. He'd confessed that he was married and that had been the end of the affair. After the first shock of his deceit and the realisation that she was faced with the prospect of becoming a single mother, Annabel had rallied and had been looking forward to having a child of her own. Since she'd lost it the days were empty and her heart like a stone.

It was the reason why she'd moved north to get away from painful memories of betrayal and loss. But agonising parents such as Aaron Lewis need have no fear. Her dedication to the job was as strong as ever. No one would be able to say that she put her own heartache before that of others, and as an autumn sun poked its head through the curtains she rolled over and slept.

Lucy was awake and crying.

'My head hurts, Daddy,' she whimpered.

'Yes, I know,' Aaron said gently. 'We'll give you

something to make it feel better in a moment, Lucy, but first tell me, can you see me all right?'

She blinked weakly.

'Yes. You've got your blue shirt on.'

'Can you see Grandma?'

Without moving her head, Lucy looked sideways to where Mary was sitting.

'Yes. Why is she crying?'

'Because you're awake…and getting better.'

'What happened to me?'

Aaron took a deep breath.

'Let's see if you can remember.'

Her bruised little face was crumpled with the effort of thinking back but she didn't disappoint him.

'I fell off the climbing frame and there was something there. I banged my head on it.'

'Good girl,' he said gently, and his mother's tears turned to smiles. 'The doctor who mended your poorly head is coming to see you and then we'll give you something to make it feel better.'

It was the same as before. He heard the door behind him open and shut and she was standing beside him, the pale-faced doctor who had been there for Lucy when he hadn't been.

'Hello, Lucy,' she said quietly. 'How are you feeling?'

'My head hurts,' she said fretfully.

'I'm sure that it does. You gave it a nasty knock and I had to put you together again like they tried to do for Humpty Dumpty. Sister is going to give you something to stop it hurting and a nice cool drink. Then later on we'll take some pictures of your head.'

'Will *that* hurt?' Lucy asked.

'We'll be very gentle,' Annabel promised, then turned

to the tall figure beside her. 'Does she remember what happened?'

'Yes, thank goodness.'

His eyes were moist and if he hadn't been Head of Paediatrics she would have put a comforting hand out to him, but she'd never operated on the child of a top doctor before, she thought wryly, and didn't know what the rules were.

Aaron's glance had switched to his mother.

'Go home and get some rest,' he told her gently. 'You've had an anxious time. I wish you could have been spared it. The folks in Reception will get you a taxi and I'll use your car when I come home, which will be a while yet.'

'All right,' she agreed, getting to her feet. 'Now that I've seen Lucy awake I feel better.' Planting a kiss on her granddaughter's bruised cheek, she went.

As a nurse gave the little girl something for the pain and a drink in a cup with a spout so that she didn't have to move, Annabel said, 'You are lucky to have such a wonderful mother. Does she live with you?'

He was staring at her with raised brows and she felt her cheeks reddening. Aaron Lewis must think her extremely nosy, she thought as she fiddled with her stethoscope and pushed back a strand of hair off her brow.

It seemed an eternity before he spoke and then he said, 'Yes, my mother *is* wonderful and, yes, she does live with us. Having her there helps to make up for Lucy's mother not being around any more.'

If he was expecting her to start asking questions about that after her first display of curiosity he was very much mistaken, she decided. Though by now she *was* intrigued.

It would all come out eventually as they were going

to be working together, most of the time in close proximity. Aaron and his team were involved in diagnosis
and treatment, while the other surgeons and herself performed the necessary surgery that would bring their
small patients back to health. And for those who were
not so lucky, a better quality of life...

Aaron was still there late that evening. He wasn't offi-
cially on duty for a couple of days, which would have
given him time to relax before going back to Barnaby's,
but all that had changed and Annabel thought that, jet-
lagged or not, this man was staying put until he was
happy about his daughter's condition.

A junior doctor and a relief surgeon from the General
Hospital were due to come on duty at ten o'clock and
that would be the routine until the other two regulars
came back.

Aaron had been by Lucy's side while further scans
had been done to check on the success of the operation,
and soon they would know whether the man who was
seeing the other face of medicine, from the position of
anxious parent, could relax.

Annabel didn't know why but she felt an affinity with
him. Maybe it was because she'd recently suffered a
great loss herself and had known the aching grief that
had come with the knowledge that *her* baby would never
see the light of day.

She'd dealt with grieving and frantic parents since
then but had never felt like this, and she told herself it
must be because they were both doctors seeing life from
the opposite side of the fence.

The results came through just as she was due to go
off duty at ten o'clock and as they studied them the two
doctors were smiling. The skull was as back to normal

in shape and size as it could be so soon after surgery. There was no bleeding and the bone fragments were still in place where she'd repaired them.

When he turned to her there was warmth in his eyes for the first time and he said abruptly, 'I think some thanks are overdue, Dr Swain. Charles Drury, who I hold in high esteem, couldn't have done better.'

She smiled and he thought that with a bit more life in her and some natural colour in her cheeks this hazel-eyed doctor would be quite something. His glance went to her hands. There was no wedding ring on view. But that didn't mean anything these days. She could have a partner. Though that wasn't likely if she was living in the soulless block in the hospital grounds.

There was a solitariness about her. The air of a loner. Curiosity was stirring in him, but he wasn't going to let her see it. He would find out soon enough what was going on in her life if they were going to be teaming up on the wards.

She was ready to leave and Aaron was still sitting beside a sleeping Lucy.

'I'm finished for the day, Dr Lewis,' she said quietly. 'But if you need me at all during the night, call me. A junior doctor and a surgeon on loan from the General are taking over now, but Lucy is *my* patient and I want it to stay that way.'

He nodded, almost asleep himself as jet-lag was beginning to take over.

'Why don't you go home for a couple of hours?' she suggested. 'It must be quite some time since you slept. I believe you've been on a tour of paediatric hospitals in America and were met at the airport with news of Lucy's accident.'

'I suppose I could pop home for an hour,' he was

saying. 'I need a shower and a change of clothes, and at the moment all is quiet with Lucy so, yes, Dr Swain, I'll take your advice.'

'The name is Annabel,' she told him.

Again he was aware of her in a strange sort of way.

'Suits you,' he commented briefly. 'At least it would if…'

His voice had trailed away and with a wry smile she finished the sentence for him, 'I wasn't such a washed-out mess?'

For the first time in ages she was bothered about what someone thought of her.

It was Aaron's turn to smile.

'That isn't how I would describe you. It would be more along the lines of someone who looks as if they need plenty of rest and vitamins. Have you been ill recently?'

'No,' she said, not sure if a painful miscarriage came into that category.

'So it must just be due to the strains and stresses of health care that get to us all at one time or another,' he commented, and with nothing further to say she nodded.

When Annabel had gone, Aaron did as she'd suggested and drove the short distance to the house that he and Eloise had bought when they'd married. She'd loved the rambling red-brick place and coming back to it without her after that disastrous holiday had been dreadful, but, as his mother had said, life had to go on and, as Lucy was growing older, his mother's stoic calm and his daughter's laughter had made it into a home again.

The luxury in which he lived was a far cry from Annabel Swain's living quarters, he thought as he put his key in the lock. What was a woman like her doing in hospital accommodation, for heaven's sake?

His mother was in bed but not asleep, and the moment she heard his step on the landing she came out to ask about Lucy.

'So far so good,' he told her. 'She's rational, as you saw when she awoke, and the surgery that Annabel Swain performed was spot on from the looks of it.'

Mary nodded.

'We owe that lady a lot, Aaron. I know that she was only doing the job she's paid to do, but I liked her the moment I saw her. She'd barely had time to get her foot over the doorstep at Barnaby's and she was operating on our precious girl. When Lucy comes home, why don't we invite her over for a meal?'

'I agree with all you say,' he told her, 'but she might think an invitation to dinner a bit over the top.'

'Nonsense!' his mother exclaimed. 'Annabel Swain looks as if she could do with some tender loving care herself. She's too thin and pale.'

Aaron was smiling. 'And you'd like to turn her into a buxom wench?'

'Not exactly. I wouldn't have thought that "buxom wenches" were quite your type.'

'What has it got to do with me?' he asked with dark brows rising. 'You're not going to try and marry me off again, are you? Because it won't work.'

'You can't mourn Eloise for ever,' she said gently.

'It has nothing to do with that. I accepted long ago that she's gone and won't be coming back. But if and when I decide to marry again, *I'll* do the choosing.'

She laughed. 'All right. I get the message, but I'm not getting any younger, you know. Lucy needs a younger woman in her life.'

'Yes, I know,' he agreed, 'and when the time is right I'll do something about it.'

He felt vaguely irritated that his mother was taking such an interest in a woman that he'd only just met. Yet he had to admit that he'd been drawn to her for some reason and there hadn't been many women he could say that about since he'd lost Eloise.

But reason said it was because she'd saved his daughter's life. It certainly wasn't because he'd been bowled over by her looks. Like a lot of other overworked doctors he'd met, she was white-faced, with dark smudges beneath those striking hazel eyes, and weary.

After he'd showered and changed Aaron unloaded his luggage from his mother's car and took out the gift he'd brought for Lucy. Mary was on the verge of sleep again, so he crept in and put the box that held a gold bracelet from one of New York's top stores on the bedside table.

He'd brought his daughter a doll, a miniature version of a pretty cheer-leader, and hoped that it might help to take her mind off the aches and pains that were the aftermath of surgery. Patti-Faye, she was called, and he thought whimsically that with her pouting red lips and glossy blonde bob she was an overstated version of the opposite sex, while the woman who had been in his thoughts was *understated* to say the least.

# CHAPTER TWO

IN THE days that followed Lucy continued to make a good recovery. There had been no worrying after-effects from the surgery and every time Aaron looked at his daughter he rejoiced.

She was home now. She would soon be back at primary school and in the meantime was once more under her grandmother's wing while Aaron was working.

He was back in harness now. On the wards and in Outpatients. He also supervised paediatric care in local clinics, referring problems to a consultant at Barnaby's.

Aaron's own speciality was neonatal problems and on a cold Monday morning he was due to see a baby boy who had been born flawless but now had an unsightly birthmark on his face.

The child had been referred from the Infirmary where the birth had taken place, and the distressed parents would be hoping he was going to wave a magic wand...

But before that he'd seen Annabel Swain coming from the direction of the accommodation blocks as he was parking his car and had sat watching her approach.

As Lucy had recovered their brief affinity had dwindled. Almost as if it had been born only of the crisis and now that it was over they'd taken stock of each other and stepped back.

It wasn't exactly that on his part, but he had to admit that he might have given Annabel the impression that she'd served her purpose as far as he was concerned and that they were back on a footing of senior paediatrician and surgeon. It wasn't the case, but now that his anxiety over Lucy was abating he was conscious that he had done nothing to further their acquaintance and she *had* saved his daughter's life.

And now here she was, hurrying along with a chill wind nipping at her ankles, snuggled inside a long winter coat, and still with the pallor that had concerned him when they'd first met.

On the occasions they'd been together during Lucy's stay in hospital he'd sensed melancholy in her and would have liked to have asked what was wrong, but had felt that he would be rebuffed if he did. After all they *were* strangers. Maybe if they'd met in the usual way of hospital staff, in a situation of a new member meeting a senior colleague and taking it from there, they would be easier with each other.

But they had been thrown together on an October morning with himself in a state of great anxiety and Annabel having spent her first hours at Barnaby's operating on his daughter. Consequently she now knew all about him, while he knew nothing of her, except that she was a cool and very competent surgeon.

She was almost level and when she saw him getting out of the car she stopped and said, 'Hello there. How's little Lucy?'

'Fine,' he said smilingly. 'And you?'

'Me?'

'Yes…you. How are you? It seems we haven't spoken of anything other than hospital business.'

'I'm all right, thank you.'

He didn't believe that, but now he saw an opportunity to get her out of that dreadful flat for a few hours.

'We wondered if you'd like to come round for a meal one night,' he said casually, and watched her eyes widen.

'My mother thought it would be one way of saying thank you for what you did for Lucy.'

So it wasn't *his* idea, she thought as her pleasure at the invitation began to evaporate.

'Thank you. That would be very nice,' she said quietly. 'I don't seem to have seen anything other than the flat, the operating theatre and the hospital grounds since I got here, but now that Mr Drury is back from his prolonged holiday and Mark Lafferty has also surfaced, I'm beginning to feel a little less pressured.'

'Would Friday be OK?' he asked, hoping that his mother hadn't got anything planned, as she would be disappointed if she couldn't be there.

'Yes. I'm not on duty and have the weekend free, so there would be no problem.'

'Good. Friday it is. Shall we say eight o'clock?'

Annabel nodded.

'Yes. Eight o'clock will be fine.'

'I'll pick you up, Annabel.'

'There's no need,' she protested. 'I have my car.'

'Yes, I know, but I'll come for you just the same. I don't like to think of you driving around in the dark in a strange town.'

She swallowed hard. It had been so long since anyone had cared whether she lived or died, it was nice to be fussed over for once.

She smiled and Aaron thought again that she would be really something if she was happy and cared for. But he wasn't going to be volunteering to bring about either of those conditions. He was content as he was with his mother and Lucy to cherish and a job he loved. He'd not forgotten his mother saying that she wasn't getting any younger, but that sort of problem could be resolved by bringing in extra help around the house.

He'd loved Eloise. She'd been an outgoing, bubbly blonde, curvy and petite. The woman standing beside him was her exact opposite. Tall, slender, *too* thin, in fact, with brown hair and eyes, and from what he'd seen so far, a restrained personality. So why did he have this curiosity regarding her?

It wasn't *that* intense, though, was it? It had taken him long enough to invite her to dinner. His mother would be surprised and pleased. She'd never mentioned inviting Annabel round after that first time but he'd sensed that the idea was still in her mind.

Mary had loved her daughter-in-law, but it didn't stop her from wanting happiness for him now, even though he'd made it clear that he wasn't in the market for a second marriage. He could imagine Annabel's expression if she knew that such an idea had entered his mother's mind.

'Right, then,' she was saying. 'If you're going to pick me up, I'm in Flat Twelve on the ground floor.'

'Ground floor?' he echoed. 'I hope there's good security.' And immediately felt that he was fussing.

'Yes, plenty,' she assured him, eyes widening in surprise. Then, with her glance switching to the big clock above the hospital entrance, she turned to go and with the thought of his outpatient clinic that was due to start shortly, Aaron did likewise.

That was a bolt from the blue, Annabel thought as she took off her coat and hung it in her locker. An invitation to dine with Aaron Lewis and his family. It would be something to look forward to in her drab existence as she had to admit that he intrigued her.

When they were in each other's proximity she found her glance on him all the time, but she supposed that he had that effect on most women. He was one of the most attractive men she'd ever seen …and the least approachable from a personal point of view.

Not workwise, though. With their small patients it was a different matter. They had that in common. Complete dedication to the children in their care. And while they were putting it into practice, the pain of what was *not* happening in the rest of her life was bearable.

The mark on the baby's face was red, round and raised. There had been no sign of it at birth. It had appeared during the first few weeks of life and now covered a large area of his tiny cheek.

Aaron recognised it immediately.

'It is a kind of haemangioma,' he told them, 'an abnormal distribution of blood vessels, commonly known as a strawberry mark. They enlarge rapidly during the first few weeks after the baby is born and will persist for six months or so, but the good news is that after that time the mark will gradually disappear. They're usually gone by the time the child is five but may take a little bit longer.'

The young mother breathed a sign of thankfulness but the baby's father wasn't so easily satisfied.

'And so what sort of treatment are you going to recommend?'

'Strawberry naevi don't usually require treatment,' Aaron told him. 'We would only remove it if the birthmark bleeds frequently, or if it is on the lip, tongue or genitals. It is done by laser treatment, but not recommended unless distress is being caused.'

The beautiful baby boy was lying contentedly in his mother's arms and Aaron said, 'Your son doesn't seem to be in any discomfort so I don't advise surgery at present. But I would like to see him every three months, and if any problems do occur don't hesitate to get back to me.'

'And so we've got to put up with him looking like this for years,' the father persisted.

'Leave it, Peter,' his wife said. 'At least we know that the birthmark is going to go eventually, and I don't want our baby to be operated on just to satisfy your male pride.'

When they'd gone Aaron thought he could see both their points of view. The young husband was no different to a lot of parents who couldn't cope with their child being different. His wife was only concerned about the baby, and rightly so.

The clinic was over. It had been the usual mixture of serious and small paediatric problems. Several of the children he'd seen today would need surgery. Annabel came to mind again and he had to tell himself that Charles and Mark were back. She wasn't going to find new zest if he started passing all his sick children to her to be operated on.

Like teenager Oliver Thomas, for instance, who was going to need brain surgery in an attempt to alleviate severe epilepsy. He would need a team of doctors for the operation that Aaron felt necessary in his case. Then there was nine-year-old James Leech. He'd seen him that morning and had suggested an operation to straighten his protruding ears.

He might have a chat with her about them on Friday night, but then thought better of it. She would think he was some bore if all he could talk about was work over dinner.

*      *      *

The moment Aaron stopped the car in front of the accommodation block on Friday night, Annabel appeared in the entrance. When he saw her he blinked.

She was wearing a cream cashmere jacket over a long black dress, with high-heeled shoes the same colour as the jacket, and carrying a matching bag.

Her hair was swept off her face and hung down her back in a shining coil, and as she drew nearer he saw in the light from the streetlamps that the pallor that worried him had been covered with light make-up.

Was this the same understated paediatric surgeon who had entered his life at the time of Lucy's accident? he asked himself as she opened the passenger door and slid into the seat beside him.

'Hello, there,' he said as she smiled across at him. 'You look…er…'

He wanted to tell her she looked wonderful, but suddenly felt she might think he was making too much out of an invitation to dinner.

She laughed. 'Not as grotty as usual, were you about to say?'

'Of course not,' he protested. 'I wouldn't be so rude.'

'But you might think it?'

'Nothing of the kind. But I'll tell you what I *do* think.'

'And what is that?'

'I think that you're hurting for some reason. I saw you this afternoon when I was examining the baby with the dislocated hips.'

He watched her face close up and knew he'd hit a nerve.

'You've no right.'

'What do you mean?'

'To be watching me.'

'I can't help it. I'm curious about you. For one thing you seem so alone.'

'That's because I am.'

'And is that how you want it to be.'

'Not particularly,' she said in a casual tone that he found irritating. 'But circumstances alter cases, just as broken noses alter faces.'

Aaron frowned.

'Obviously it *doesn't* bother you all that much or you wouldn't be so flippant about it.'

She was serious now. 'It's more a case of having to accept what life hands out to us, Aaron.'

'And what has it handed out to you?'

'Nothing good of late.'

'So I'm right. There *is* something troubling you.'

Annabel could have told him that it was there in the form of a great big lump of misery, but for some strange reason she wanted her acquaintance with Aaron Lewis to be free of past encumbrances. She didn't want him to see her as someone with poor judgement so she didn't answer.

'What about family?' he persisted, knowing he was being intrusive but unable to conceal his curiosity.

Within minutes they would be at the house. This brief moment of closeness in the car would be over and for some reason it was important to know what was going on in Annabel's life. She already knew most of what there was to know about him, but he knew nothing about her past, present or future expectations.

He was about to find out…some of it.

'My parents were archaeologists, more interested in old relics than a small child, I was fobbed off on relatives for most of my childhood and the moment I was old enough I cut free and enrolled in medical school. Not long after that they were on a dig in India when there was an earthquake. They died there, along with many others. I was almost nineteen at the time. So, you see, you are the fortunate one. You have your mother and Lucy, both of them delightful. I envy you.'

'Yes, I *am* fortunate,' he agreed, bemused by Annabel's condensed description of what must have been a miserable childhood. But he didn't feel so 'fortunate' at night in his lonely double bed.

The house was looming up in front of them and Annabel said, 'Wow! What a lovely place you've got. The flat will seem like a rabbit hutch after this.'

He smiled. 'I'm sure that you could do better. Is there a reason why you're in hospital accommodation?'

'It's only because I couldn't be bothered to go house-hunting when I got the job at Barnaby's.' As he drove onto a wide paved drive beside an immaculate garden she added, 'But after tonight I might be spurred on to greater things.'

His mother and Lucy were coming out to meet them and Annabel thought, This is unreal. What am I doing here? Aaron is doing the polite thing, showing his gratitude by inviting me to eat with them. He didn't have to do it.

When she glanced across at him there was a look on his face that she couldn't fathom, but there were other things to claim her attention. Lucy was saying shyly, 'Hello, Dr Swain.' His mother was beaming her welcome and for the first time in months Annabel was beginning to unwind.

Bending down to the little girl, she said softly. 'My name is Annabel, Lucy. No need to call me Dr Swain. That's just my hospital name.' She turned to a smiling Mary. 'It's so nice to meet you again, Mrs Lewis. I've just been telling Aaron how lucky he is to have you with him.'

Mary's smile was slipping as her glance went to her son, and Annabel sensed undercurrents. But the comment had been innocent enough and if she'd been barging in where she shouldn't, it hadn't been intentional. There was the missing wife and mother, of course. Maybe it was to do with that.

The inside of the house was just as imposing as the outside. Someone who had a feel for colour and style had been responsible, and when she commented on it, almost as if it was the opening she'd been waiting for, Mary said, 'My daughter-in-law was an interior designer. She had a feel for those sorts of things.'

'Have *you* got a mummy, Annabel?' Lucy asked suddenly.

'Er…no, I haven't,' she told the little girl, with the feeling that this evening was turning into a 'get to know you' sort of occasion. It was only minutes ago that she'd been telling Aaron about her family background, or lack of it, and now Lucy was tuning in, but Annabel wasn't prepared for what was coming next.

'*My* mummy drowned. So did my grandad.'

'Oh!' Annabel breathed. 'I am so sorry. What a terrible thing to happen.'

She was speaking to Lucy but her gaze was on Aaron standing very still beside his daughter.

'Yes, it was,' he replied tonelessly, 'but, Lucy, we haven't brought Annabel here to upset her, have we? And I'm sure that Mummy and Grandad are watching over us somewhere and hoping we have a nice evening.'

Annabel's mind was reeling. She'd been so wrapped up in her own misery and what she'd just heard had been like a bolt from the blue. She wasn't going to ask but Aaron's composure told her that the tragedy wasn't very recent and his mother was calm enough as she announced, 'The meal is almost ready, Annabel.' She glanced at her son. 'Shall we have a drink before dinner, my dear?'

'Er...yes,' he said, as if bringing his thoughts back from somewhere far away.

Lucy, quite unaware that she'd dropped a bombshell, piped up, 'And I'll have a drink of orange, please, Grandma.'

As the evening progressed the atmosphere was friendly and relaxed and Annabel thought wistfully that, whether the mother figure was missing or not, this was family life at its most enjoyable.

When it was time for Lucy to go to bed Mary said, 'We'll let Daddy off bathtime tonight, shall we, Lucy? Annabel is our guest and it is only good manners that he should entertain her while I get you ready for bed.'

Aaron was smiling, but there was a glint in his eye that puzzled Annabel, as if messages were flashing between his mother and himself, but Mary's expression was innocent enough and Lucy had no problems with the suggestion. She trotted off obediently after planting a shy kiss on Annabel's cheek.

When she'd gone Annabel said into the silence that had fallen, 'Lucy looks fine, Aaron. Are you satisfied with her progress?'

He nodded. 'Yes. I am. That was a nightmare I wouldn't want to repeat.'

'Your anguish at the time would have been understandable in any case,' she told him, 'but after hearing what happened to your wife it must have been a nightmare. Do you want to tell me about it? I've told you about myself, so perhaps it's your turn to unburden yourself.'

That wasn't exactly true. She'd only told him about her past, not the miserable present.

'I would rather we could have kept it light this evening,' he said after a moment's silence, 'but Lucy, bless her, says whatever is in her mind, like most children do, so I suppose I don't mind talking about Eloise. I think about her enough.

'We were on holiday in Cornwall and having a picnic on one of its fabulous beaches. Mum and Eloise were sunbathing and Dad was swimming out in the cove. We'd forgotten something, the sunblock cream to be exact, and I'd taken Lucy, who was only a toddler then, back to the hotel with me to get it.

'While I was gone my dad got into difficulties. He was a strong swimmer but wasn't aware of the dangerous currents there, and on seeing his distress Eloise went in after him. By the time I got back they'd gone. Swept out to sea. The next time Mum and I saw them was when their bodies were washed up further along the coast a few days later.'

'That *is* awful,' she choked.

He nodded. 'My mother thinks I should be looking for someone to take Eloise's place, that I've been on my own long enough. But who is to say that the right wife for me would be the right mother for Lucy?'

Annabel averted her gaze from his. She would have settled for being just a one-parent family, given the chance, and no child of hers would ever have been subjected to the awful feeling of rejection that had tarnished her life. But she understood what this caring father was saying.

'I would imagine that is a problem that faces many single parents when they consider remarrying,' she said slowly, 'but a child can be just as miserable with its birth parents as with someone not of its own blood. I don't know you all that well, Aaron, but you strike me as a person who would rarely make a wrong decision, either in your work or in your personal life, because you are cool and calm in everything you do.'

She wasn't to know that he was feeling anything but cool and calm at that moment. She was getting to him as no other woman had since he'd lost Eloise, and it was much more than just sexual chemistry.

In the car earlier she'd told him about her loveless childhood and he'd wanted to hold her close and soothe away the hurt from a friendship point of view, nothing more. And now, with a wisdom that no doubt came from her own experience, she was putting him right about his own life. Making him see that it *could* be possible to find happiness with someone else.

Sitting beside him with cheeks warming at her own temerity, Annabel was facing up to the fact that she liked this man a lot. She'd had respect for him from the moment of their meeting, even though on that awful morning he'd been brusque and dubious of her capabilities. But now it was something deeper than that. To compare Randy Graham with Aaron would be like putting a fake next to the real thing.

It wouldn't be wise to let her feelings run away with her, though. The fact that they were having this discussion showed that Aaron saw her as merely someone to talk to. He would never have said what he had if he'd any yearnings towards her. And was it surprising? He must see her as the person she had become, a washed-out, grieving loner, and for the first time in months she wanted to be different.

Aaron was smiling to conceal his own thoughts.

'I don't know about me. But you have a wisdom all

of your own. It's good to be able to talk to someone who understands.' He took her hand in his and gave it a gentle squeeze.

It was just a friendly gesture, but she felt some of the chill leave her blood and for a crazy moment wondered what it would be like to sit in this charming room with him every evening after a hard day on the wards and in Theatre, with Lucy sleeping contentedly above.

His mother came in at that moment carrying a tray with coffee and pastries on it, and Aaron got to his feet.

'Lucy is waiting for a goodnight kiss,' she said, smiling up at him. 'I won't pour the coffee until you come down.'

When he'd gone Mary said, 'And how are things with you, Dr Swain? Are you settling in all right in your new surroundings?'

Annabel wasn't sure whether she was referring to the dismal flat or Barnaby's itself, so she just said, 'Yes, fine, thank you, Mrs Lewis. And it's not Dr Swain when I'm out and about. It's Annabel.'

Aaron's mother smiled. 'And my name is Mary,' she said, straightening an imaginary crease in her skirt with a plump hand. 'So what do you think of my son?'

Annabel's eyes widened. What was that supposed to mean?

'I don't know Aaron all that well, er…Mary, but from what I've seen of him I think he is a doting father and a good doctor.'

'I keep telling him he should marry again,' the other woman said wistfully. 'I won't be here for ever and…' She'd left the sentence unfinished but it made her concerns clear.

'I can understand how you feel,' Annabel told her, squirming inwardly, 'but that is up to him, isn't it?'

They could hear his feet on the stairs and Mary sighed. 'Yes, I suppose you're right. We're happy enough as we are, but the future does worry me sometimes.'

Not as much as it worries me, Annabel thought wryly, but their anxieties had different sources. *She* would be happy if she could find some direction in her life. Except for the job that she adored it was empty, and likely to remain so, with the hurt inside her that Aaron seemed to be so strangely aware of.

Maybe she should have told him her problems in return for him telling her his. He might have had some words of wisdom to impart, but her feelings were still too raw to bring out into the open and where his loss had been due to a cruel twist of fate, hers had been self-inflicted up to a point. She was a doctor, for heaven's sake, and should have taken better precautions against pregnancy. Instead of letting her longing for a child overcome common sense.

As Aaron drove her home Annabel was thinking that it had been a strange and unsettling evening. She'd been allowed into the warm circle of a close family, depleted though they were, and at the same time had experienced the pleasure to be had from gracious living.

Maybe it had done her some good, seeing how other people lived. If it had lifted her out of the doldrums, Aaron would have done her a favour by inviting her to his home.

But before leaving him she had to get one thing clear. She was certain there had been no ulterior motive when he had mentioned the problems of remarriage, but she had a strong feeling that his mother's remarks had been aimed differently. That she had been sounding her out as a prospective candidate for the position of second wife and stepmother to Lucy.

Grateful for the shadowy interior of the car and aware that they would be back at the flat within minutes, she said casually, 'While you were upstairs with Lucy I got the impression that your mother was vetting me for the marriage market.'

He groaned and, taking his eyes off the road for a moment, scrutinised her face, searching for a guide to her feelings on the matter.

'I'm sorry about that, Annabel,' he said quietly. 'She means well, but Mum is letting her anxieties about the future take over. I invited you to dine with us as a thank you for what you did for Lucy.'

So let's get that straight, he seemed to be saying, and she had to admit she was just a bit disappointed. Was she so muted down and drab that he didn't see anything attractive about her?

When he stopped the car in front of the flats she turned to him and said softly, 'It's been a lovely evening, Aaron. I've really enjoyed it. Thank you so much for inviting me.'

He observed her with an eyebrow raised questioningly.

'What? In spite of having to listen to my problems and then having my mother follow them up with her broad hints about my solitary state? For all she knew, you might be married or already have someone in your life. Have you?'

His tone had been apologetic, but that last question had come like a bullet from a gun, as if her answer was going to matter.

'No. I haven't,' she told him, not knowing whether to be annoyed or amused at the question. 'I'm not married, engaged, in a partnership or anything else. Being alone has its advantages. I'm free to do whatever I please.'

'But you haven't always been alone, have you?' he asked, amazed how relieved he was to know she was free.

'No. I haven't. But I am now.'

Aaron said no more. There was something in the tone of her voice that told him not to pursue it. Instead, he asked in a lighter tone. 'Well? Are you going to ask me in?'

She smiled. 'No. I'm not. I know you're bursting to see the inside of my rabbit hutch, but I don't think it would be a good idea.'

'Why not?'

'Because you have some preconceived idea that it's going to be dreadful.'

'Right, then. I'd better be off. Have a nice weekend, Annabel,' he said, adding with a boyish grin that was oddly appealing. 'Keep taking the vitamins.'

As she was opening the passenger door of the car he leaned across and kissed her lightly on the cheek. As she gazed at him in surprise he said, 'Just a kiss between friends. Nothing to do with the marriage market.' And leaving her standing beside the door of the accommodation complex he drove off.

She'd seen another side to Aaron tonight, Annabel told herself as she lay on her hard single bed in the flat's bedroom. The brisk mantle of efficiency that he wore at Barnaby's had fallen from his shoulders and he'd let her see that he had his problems just like anyone else.

It was a terrible thing that had happened to his family. He and Mary had both suffered a double tragedy. Aaron had lost his wife and father and his mother her husband and daughter-in-law.

They'd been taken from them in a matter of minutes and he must have wished a thousand times that he'd never gone back to the hotel. But as they were both well aware, lots of people would do lots of things differently if they could see into the future.

If she'd known the misery she was letting herself in for when she'd been attracted by a lazy smile and an even lazier accent, *she* would have behaved differently. Husband-stealer she was not, and Randy had shown himself to be much less of a man than she'd thought he was when it had all come out.

It was strange how one man could deceive his wife without batting an eyelid and another should still be grieving for a woman who had died four long years ago.

Yet that was how it was. Aaron had made it painfully plain that he had no designs on her. To such an extent that she almost wished he had.

She sympathised with his mother's efforts on his behalf but he shouldn't be put in the humiliating position of advertising for a wife. It was a cold-blooded procedure and although he had barely touched her, something told her that when Aaron took a new wife, if he ever did, there would be nothing cold-blooded about it.

# CHAPTER THREE

IF HE'D been light-hearted back there at the flats Aaron was not so as he drove home. Annabel wasn't the only one thinking it had been an unsettling evening. He felt that they'd all behaved out of character except Lucy.

For his own part, his interest in the doctor who'd saved Lucy's life had increased rather than diminished while she'd been their guest. He'd seen her in a new light. For one thing, she'd taken trouble with her appearance. He didn't flatter himself that it had been on his account, but it had certainly registered, and for another, he'd admired the dignified brevity with which she'd described her family life while within the loving circle that was his.

Annabel had been like a flower opening up before his eyes and he hoped that she wouldn't have closed up again when they met on the wards at Barnaby's on Monday.

He'd had no intention of burdening her with his past and present griefs, but Lucy and his mother had set the ball rolling and he'd had to say something. Once he'd started it had been oddly comforting to be talking to an outsider who'd listened with sympathy and understanding, while making no demands on him.

And an 'outsider' Annabel must have certainly felt when he'd been so keen to emphasise that she'd been there merely in the role of someone to whom thanks were due. She must have thought him tactless and rude, though she'd shown no sign of it.

And then there'd been his mother! Sounding Annabel out and showing how anxious she was for him to find himself another wife, when he had no such intentions. It wasn't like her. She was the kindest and most thoughtful of mortals. But something had got into her and they were going to have to talk it through.

All was silent as he let himself back into the house and as he stripped off and flung himself on top of the covers of his bed Annabel's face kept coming to mind.

'No. I haven't got anyone in my life,' she'd told him back there in the car, and he'd known immediately that that hadn't always been the case. Had it been a past relationship that had taken the colour from her cheeks?

Whatever it was, he had a strong feeling that if he'd become more interested in her during the evening, his mother's comments would have put the flattener on any stirrings Annabel might have been experiencing. If she gave him a wide berth on Monday morning, he wouldn't be surprised...

But he was to see her again before Monday. On Saturday afternoon Aaron took Lucy into the town for some new shoes, and as they were leaving the shop he saw Annabel cross the road, looking in the window of an estate agent.

'We meet again,' he said from behind her a few seconds later, and she swung round in surprise.

'Yes, we do,' she agreed, adding with a special smile for Lucy, who was fishing her new shoes out of the bag for her to see, 'You'll be surprised to see that I'm looking at property.'

'Yes. What has prompted that?'

She had a smile for him now and Aaron thought if she *had* been upset the night before it obviously hadn't persisted.

'What do you think?' she replied. 'Going back to the flat after spending the evening in your palatial residence.'

'Really? So last night did do you *some* good.'

She could have told him that she'd also woken up feeling ready to face the day, which had to be a step in the right direction, and that the carrier bag she was holding held some smart new clothes. But it wouldn't do for Aaron to think he'd had *that* much influence on her.

Lucy was dangling a pair of black school shoes under her nose and Annabel bent to admire them.

'So do I take it that you'll soon be going back to school?' she said as eyes blue as the sky looked up into hers.

'Yes,' Lucy said. 'On Monday. I've been away a long time. I'll be behind in my work and all my friends will have forgotten me.'

'I've told Lucy that the teacher knows she had a nasty accident and won't expect her to catch up straight away,' Aaron said gravely as his eyes met hers above Lucy's blonde head.

'Yes, of course,' Annabel agreed, 'and I'm sure that your friends won't have forgotten you. I imagine that they all think you very brave having such a serious operation and coming back to school looking just the same as before.'

'Can I tell them that the doctor who mended my head is my friend?'

'Er…yes, by all means,' Annabel said, aware of the amusement in Aaron's dark eyes. She watched it change to surprise as she suggested, 'Maybe we could take Lucy's class on a tour of the hospital. It would increase her standing and they would know what to expect if ever any of them have to be admitted.'

'Good thinking!' he exclaimed. 'I'm sure that she would love to show them where you ''mended'' her head. But getting back to your house-hunting. Have you seen anything that appeals to you?'

'Not yet. I'd like something small and classy with open views.'

'There's a small coach house for sale next door to my place,' he said. 'It isn't cheap, but it's certainly classy.'

He could have gone on to say, It belongs to a friend of mine who spends a lot of time abroad. When he's away I show prospective buyers round. But he was already wishing he hadn't spoken.

For one thing his mother would be sure to read something into the suggestion, even though it had been totally spontaneous, and Annabel also might think it came from what had been said the previous evening. So instead he followed it up with, 'Though on second thoughts I think it would be too big for you.'

'No harm in having a look though, is there?' she said with her newfound enthusiasm carrying her along.

'No. I suppose not,' he agreed reluctantly. 'You could ring the agent and ask for a viewing.'

'Supposing I like it,' she said slowly, aware that he was having second thoughts, 'how would you feel having me living next door? Seeing me all day at the hospital and having me almost on your doorstep for the rest of the time.'

'It wouldn't bother me,' he replied unconvincingly. 'There's a high hedge between the two properties and we don't see much of the present owner.'

'That's because Uncle Richard is always away,' Lucy chipped in. 'Why can't *you* show Annabel round his house, Daddy? Like you do with all the other people?'

Annabel had to hand it to him. Aaron had been caught

out but he didn't bat an eyelid. He merely said, 'If Annabel wants to view Uncle Richard's house, Lucy, she is better seeing it with someone she doesn't know. I wouldn't want to influence her.'

'I think you already have,' she told him coolly. 'Maybe I'll give it a miss after all.'

She bent and kissed Lucy's soft cheek.

'I'll be thinking of you on Monday,' she told her. 'I hope you have a good day and I won't forget what I said about your class being shown round the hospital.'

For her father Annabel had a curt nod.

'I'll be seeing you, Aaron,' she said, and he knew from the tone of her voice that it was more of a threat than a promise.

You certainly handled that well, he told himself as he walked Lucy back to the car. It was your suggestion that Annabel look at Richard's house, but the words were barely out of your mouth before you were backing off. Go on at this rate and she'll be thinking she's got something catching. If you wanted to put her off you made a first-class job of it. For someone who always knows exactly where he's heading, you're acting like an indecisive ditherer.

It was Sunday afternoon and a boisterous wind was lifting the dead leaves in the garden of the house next door as Aaron stared thoughtfully through his study window.

Richard Clements, who lived there, was a television producer and often away. He would appear out of the blue, then a couple of days later be off on his travels again.

He was unmarried, which Aaron often thought was just as well. For any woman he took up with would be left alone for long periods while he was working. Yet he always seemed to have some female company around when he came home for one of his brief stays.

The winter dusk was falling and as Aaron was about to turn away the lights came on suddenly next door. His eyes widened when he saw Richard framed in the window opposite and with him, of all people, was Annabel.

So he hadn't put her off, he thought incredulously. She was doing the opposite to what he'd expected, viewing Richard's house. If the russet-haired charmer who was his friend and neighbour was on his usual form, she would be eating out of his hand.

And what if she was? It was nothing to do with him. After the way he'd behaved the previous day she probably thought he had a hidden agenda regarding the place himself, and didn't want her muscling in. And with that thought in mind she'd arranged to view the property, just to let him see that she was not to be manipulated.

He was right about that. Talk about keep away from me and mine, Annabel had thought as he'd disappeared amongst the Saturday shoppers with Lucy holding tightly to his hand. She'd decided to arrange a viewing of the house next to his to let him see she had a mind of her own. With the thought had come the deed.

And now here she was being shown round by its owner, who had explained that he'd returned from France an hour ago and would soon be off again.

'That's why I'm selling,' Richard Clements was saying as he led the way to the upper floor of the coach house. 'I'm too much of a rolling stone to have a place like this left empty.'

'It's a beautiful house,' she murmured. 'A colleague of mine lives next door.'

'Aaron, you mean?' he exclaimed in surprise. 'So what are you? A nurse? Doctor?'

'I'm a paediatric surgeon.'

'And how well do you know him?'

'Not well at all,' she told him with feeling, and changed the subject by asking when he could move out if she was interested.

He shrugged.

'Whenever. Once I get a buyer I'll fit in with them.'

When the tour of the house was over Annabel said, 'Thanks for showing me round, Mr Clements. If I'm interested I'll get in touch with the agent.'

'Sure,' he said easily. 'Or tell Aaron. He knows how to get in touch with me if I'm not around. You and he aren't an item are you?'

'No. Certainly not.'

'Right, then. So do you fancy coming to have dinner with me? I'm starving.'

'No, thanks. I have another couple of properties to view.'

It wasn't strictly true. She *had* made arrangements to see two other houses, but not that afternoon. She was refusing because this man was a confident charmer and she'd had her fill of that type. Also, she was beginning to feel a bit guilty. What would Aaron think when he knew she'd been shown round this place after he'd tried to discourage her?

That she had a mind of her own maybe.

On Monday morning Aaron received a cool greeting from Annabel when they met on the wards and he countered with, 'I saw you viewing Richard Clements's house yesterday. What did you think of it?'

'Very nice.'

'And?'

'And nothing. I've got others to see in different areas. He was very pleasant—charming, in fact.'

'Yes. Rick is a nice guy,' he agreed, wishing once again that he'd never mentioned the house next door. The last thing Annabel needed was a seasoned ladies' man like his friend.

But that was only *his* opinion. Maybe she had other ideas and if she had, what had it got to do with him? Yet he was peeved. It was typical of the life he led that he should be fighting shy of any new commitments, while his friend wouldn't hesitate to proposition Annabel within minutes of meeting if the mood took him.

'It's a wonder he didn't ask you out. Richard doesn't let the grass grow under his feet,' he told her with a facial contortion meant to be a smile.

'He did,' she said casually, as if she saw nothing strange in it.

He tutted.

'I might have known.'

Without further comment he led the way to their first patient of the day. Teenager Oliver Thomas was being prepared for his neurosurgery, which would hopefully reduce his convulsions.

Charles Drury had come to join them as he would be in charge of the operation, with Annabel and Mark Lafferty assisting.

When Aaron had suggested the operation to the boy's parents he'd had to warn them that there would be no guarantee of success. Yet they'd still told him to go ahead as the frequency of the convulsions and Oliver's violence towards anyone near him when they occurred was creating a situation that was unbearable for all concerned.

And now it was the day of his operation and his

mother and father would have many anxious hours of waiting ahead of them, which might end with an improvement in Oliver's condition, or the boy being in a worse state than before...

When they stopped at the next bed Aaron said in a low voice, 'We have ALD here. It's rare, genetic and often incurable, as we all know. The family are devastated, needless to say. I saw young Jack here in my clinic. His GP had sent him to me with severe vomiting, low blood-sugar levels and periods of unconsciousness. We did some tests, discovered that the adrenal glands weren't working properly and diagnosed adrenoleuko-dystrophy.

'You'll maybe remember the film *Lorenzo's Oil* where the parents never gave up trying to find a cure for their son who had this same genetic disorder. Eventually they found a combination of oils that lowered the fatty acids in the blood, which is vital in delaying the progression of ALD.

'The medical profession has never been sure whether it works or not, but the couple in the film were adamant that their son did show some improvement, and though it was many years ago, as far as I know he's still alive.

'When the illness has been diagnosed in its early stage, a bone-marrow transplant has been an option and I think we should consider it in Jack's case, if we can find a suitable donor. In the meantime, I'm putting my faith in Lorenzo's Oil.'

Charles Drury nodded.

'We're keeping him under close observation at the moment,' Aaron told them, and with a smile for the boy and a gentle pat on the head, they moved on to the next bed.

Aaron was aware of Annabel's gaze on him and it

was softer than it had been during their earlier greeting.
If he couldn't get it right in their private lives, at least
they were in tune here at Barnaby's, he thought with
spirits lifting.

As the day took its course Oliver was taken down to
Theatre with a last hug for his anxious parents and then
the waiting began.

As the surgical team scrubbed up Annabel was tense
and totally focused. She'd specialised in paediatric neu-
rological problems, but the decision to operate had been
made by Aaron and Charles Drury before she'd come to
Barnaby's and the main anxiety was going to rest on
their shoulders.

It was a no-choice situation if Oliver was going to
have any quality of life, but what they were planning to
do was dangerous. If he came through the operation suc-
cessfully, they would discover in the days that followed
if it had been worth taking the risk.

On occasions such as this every other thought was put
to one side. In their hands lay a child's life. She knew
only too well that there was nothing worse for a doctor
to leave at the end of the day knowing that a life they'd
tried to save had been lost.

It was evening. Oliver had come through the operation
and was now in the recovery unit, but Aaron's expression was still anxious as he stood beside his bed.

'So far so good, eh, Annabel?' he said as she pushed
a strand of hair back off her brow. 'I'll want to go and
bang my head against the wall if there's no improvement
after this.'

'At least we've tried,' she told him with a tired smile.
'We've done all we can. Let's hope that nature isn't

going to let us down. What time are you due to go off duty?'

'Soon, but I want to stay on a bit to make sure that the boy surfaces all right when the anaesthetic wears off. Charles and I were the ones who suggested the surgery to his parents and although they didn't need much persuading, I feel very much responsible. You're off now, are you?'

'Yes. Mr Drury is still on the premises so I'm not needed any more. I'm going for a meal.'

'Oh? Who with? Not Richard Clements, I hope.' The question was out before he'd considered how officious it was going to sound.

She sighed.

'No. If you must know, I'm eating with Mark.'

She was making a big thing out of going for a snack with a colleague after long hours of surgery, but couldn't resist teasing Aaron. What did he take her for? Or had he sized her up already? Guessed that she'd already once been too eager to get close to a man she'd trusted...and where had *that* got her? She'd shed no tears for him, but had cried her heart out for the baby she'd lost.

'He's old enough to be your father!' Aaron protested.

'What does that matter if I'm happy in his company?' she replied perversely. 'I said that we were *eating* together...not *sleeping*! What is the matter with you, Aaron? One moment you're warning me off, keeping me at a distance, and the next you're acting as if *you* were my father.'

As he faced up to the fact that *fatherly* was the last thing he felt toward this doctor, Aaron's mind was in turmoil. He was watching her slowly break out of the drab chrysallis of misery that had encased her when they'd first met and the effect it was having on him was amazing.

She was the opposite to Eloise in every way and yet he couldn't get her out of his mind. Maybe it was because she wasn't falling over herself to get to him. In the last four years there'd been a few women who'd pursued him and he'd wanted none of it. But Annabel had a sort of take-it-or-leave-it air about her that had him hooked, and if he didn't stop behaving like an interfering busybody the relationship was going to fizzle out before it had even got going.

'And so what was it that you and Aaron were discussing so seriously just before we left the hospital?' Mark asked quizzically as they ate the offerings of a nearby burger bar.

'He was warning me off older men,' she told him laughingly.

'What? Aaron was warning you about me?' he said, joining in her amusement. 'The cheek of the guy. Though it doesn't sound like him. The head of Paediatrics keeps himself to himself with regard to *his* private life and rarely interferes in ours. But it would seem that he's out to save *you* from the wolves. Though I feel it's hardly an accurate description of a fifty-year-old bachelor whose boat is the only thing that makes his pulse beat faster. Every spare moment I get I'm down at the coast.'

He was an amiable, unfussy sort of man and she could believe him when he said that sailing filled his life. He was as likely to make a pass at her as volunteer for a mission to Mars.

It was weird. From being manless for months she was now coming into contact with all types of the species.

Richard Clements, the fast worker. Mark, sitting beside her, who was in love with his boat...and Aaron. What kind of man was he? She wished she knew.

On the outside he came over as cool and clever. A loving family man, but wary. What of, she wasn't sure, but if she had to make a guess she would say it was herself.

Why, though, for heaven's sake? She'd done nothing to make him so. He'd met her while she'd been at her lowest ebb, at her least attractive, and devoid of purpose.

She wouldn't have expected him to give her a second glance and she didn't think he had until the other night when he'd invited her to dine at his house. It had been the beginning of her return to normality, but ever since he'd been as prickly as a hedgehog.

When Aaron left the hospital that night Oliver was conscious and in a stable condition. It was now a case of wait and see. His mother, grey with weariness, had said, 'It was a terrible decision to have to make, Dr Lewis, but we really had come to the end of our strength and so had Oliver. If it turns out that we were wrong then we'll have to live with it, but at least we tried to give our son a better life and we'll be forever grateful to yourself and the other doctors for helping us towards that.'

He went home feeling unusually emotional and when Lucy met him at the door, ready for bed in her nightdress and clutching the doll he'd brought her back from America, he picked her up and held her close.

It wasn't all that long ago since *he'd* been in the terrible limbo of a parent whose child might die or suffer severe disability, and within the recollection was

Annabel, tired and white-faced yet cool and calm. A rock to hang on to.

Was that why he was fascinated by her? Gratitude? No. It was more than that, much more. The turn of her head, the soft line of her throat, the beautiful hazel eyes. When he'd picked her up the other night he'd seen her for what she really could be, and it had taken his breath away.

But instead of the evening being light-hearted and up-beat it had turned out to be a time of harking back to the past on both their parts, and for his mother's anxious thoughts about the future.

She was here now, smiling across at him as he hugged his daughter to him, and tenderness washed over him. She never did anything but what she thought would benefit Lucy and himself, and if sometimes they saw things in a different light, what did it matter?

He was feeling restless and on edge and knew the feelings weren't going to go away until he'd seen Annabel, though what excuse he could give for calling he didn't know. That was if she was back from her meal with Lafferty.

Lucy was asleep and his mother was dozing beside the fire when he came into the sitting room with his coat on.

'I'm popping out for half an hour,' he told her, and she nodded drowsily.

There was a light on in the flat and he thought that at least Annabel was in. What sort of a reception he would get was another matter.

When she saw him standing there Aaron thought she was going to close the door, and he said with a quirky smile, 'Am I going to have to put one foot inside like the bailiffs do?'

She stepped back to let him in but wasn't returning the smile.

'What do you want, Aaron?' she said levelly. 'Have you come to see if I'm behaving myself with Mark? Were you expecting me to answer the door in a satin nightdress or something? If you were, I'm sorry to disappoint you. I haven't got one. I wear an old T-shirt in bed, which ought to tell you something.'

'I haven't come to discuss your sleeping habits,' he told her, serious now. 'I'm here to apologise for what I said earlier this evening about Mark and you.'

'We went our separate ways at eight o'clock, if you must know,' she told him in the same level tone. 'He to drool over his boat and I to put the washing-machine on. But do sit down now that you're here. Your wish is granted. You're actually inside the rabbit hutch. If you wish to complain to the authorities on my behalf, feel free to do so.'

He took her hand in his and looked down at the long, capable fingers that could wield a scalpel with such precision. 'We're not getting anywhere, are we?' he said in a low voice.

Annabel was acutely conscious of his nearness. The clean male smell of him. The physique that made heads turn, the dark searching glance that seemed to see right into her soul. But it didn't, did it? Otherwise he would know that she hadn't enough zest in her to respond to what he was saying.

'Is that what you want?' she asked weakly. 'For us to *get somewhere*?'

It was laughable, he thought. He'd been told that he

was seen as a good catch by the female staff at Barnaby's, but not by this one, it would seem.

'Possibly,' he told her drily. 'But don't get too excited about the idea. I've been trying to fight it, but I seem to keep coming back for more.'

'More of what?'

'Being with you… This, maybe.'

He'd swivelled round and was reaching out for her, and the next moment his mouth was on hers. He had one hand in the hollow of her back and the other was wrapped in her hair. Her breasts were hard up against his chest, her thighs beginning to ache, and Annabel knew in those moments that this was what had been missing with Randy.

She'd mistaken what they'd had for real passion and it was taking this charismatic widower to show her the difference. But Aaron was an idealist. If she let this wonderful chemistry that was springing up between them take over, one day she might have to watch disillusion take its place.

'It's too soon,' she said, easing herself out of his arms. 'We haven't known each other five minutes.'

It was the first excuse she could think of and would have to do. The fact that she felt as if she'd known him always was not going to get an airing. Aaron had told her in his own words that he was in no hurry to marry again and yet here he was, stirring her dormant senses, making her blood run warm again.

There were two reasons why it had to stop. The first was that maybe he *was* like Randy. That he'd meant what he'd said about not marrying again, but wasn't amiss to a bit on the side. And secondly, if that wasn't the case and he really was sincere, she didn't want him to see her as less than the woman he wanted her to be.

'So what is it?' he asked. 'You've just responded to me like I never dreamed possible and now you're drawing back. You are the first woman I've touched since losing Eloise. Doesn't that tell you something?'

'Yes, it does,' she told him bleakly. 'It tells me that you have high expectations of me. Expectations that I might not be able to live up to.'

He was angry now.

'That's a lame excuse if ever I heard one. There's something you're not telling me and until I know what it is I'm groping in the dark. Or maybe you think that *groping* is what it's all about!'

He was on his feet, towering over her, and as she looked up at him, Annabel knew that Aaron deserved to know the truth. So that he could make his own judgement and, for a man who'd been celibate for four long years because of his love for a courageous woman, her own sorry tale would make distasteful hearing.

# CHAPTER FOUR

BUT the words were sticking in her throat. Those moments in Aaron's arms had been like a glimpse of the promised land after months in the wilderness. Did she want to spoil this tender thing that was shooting up between them? Maybe if their relationship was given the chance to put down some roots, her past wouldn't sound so grim when she told him.

So instead she explained lamely, 'It's how I feel, Aaron. We haven't known each other long…and I *am* afraid I might not come up to your expectations.'

His smile was tight. 'You came up to my expectations a few moments ago.'

Annabel could feel her colour rising.

'I don't mean in that way. I was referring to the difference in our lives. You have a stable, financially comfortable background and mine is far from that. I think my insecurities stem from my pillar-to-post sort of childhood. I never had the opportunity to establish myself in one place and if the chance came now I wouldn't know how to go about it.'

He sighed.

'Why do I feel that you're making excuses? *I'm* the one who should be having doubts. I have Lucy to think about…*and* my mother. I owe her a lot, and with that thought in mind I need to be going. I told her I would only be out a matter of minutes. Maybe you're right in what you say, Annabel. I shouldn't have come.'

'What was she like?' she asked, as he turned to go.

He swivelled round to face her again.

'Who?'

'Your wife.'

'Small, blonde, bubbly.'

'So I'm nothing like her. A tall, brunette, whose fizz has gone flat.'

'A good shake-up usually brings it back.'

'Not always.'

'Look, Annabel,' he said impatiently, 'I'm tired of listening to you talk in riddles. Let me know when you're ready for some plain speaking. In the meantime, goodnight.'

You're a glutton for punishment, Annabel told herself when he'd gone. That man is something else! And you've just fobbed him off. What is the matter with you? He's in a different league to Randolph Graham. Way above him in looks, stature, integrity...*and* the way he kisses. So why put a dampener on him?

It was a good question and she didn't know the true answer. Or maybe she did. The sadness she'd felt when they told her she'd miscarried was still there like a dull ache inside her.

She'd longed for a child, vowing as the wonder of her pregnancy had taken hold that it would never be made to feel unwanted as she had been. Even after Randy had made his uncomfortable confession, her joy at the coming birth had kept her spirits from falling too far. Until the day when she'd been hurrying to Theatre to deal with an emergency and had slipped.

Yet she *was* coming alive again and it was because of the man who'd just left her with his mind in a state of irritation and confusion. They were both as bad as each other. She was like a seesaw. No sooner had her life taken an upward thrust than it was plunging back down again, and as for Aaron, he was just as unpredictable.

Less than a week ago he had made it clear he had no wish to remarry and yet tonight he'd made no bones about the fact that he was attracted to her. But that didn't have to mean that he was considering her for the role of the second Mrs Lewis. Lots of men were interested in sex, but weren't necessarily rushing to put a ring on the woman's finger.

Though something told her he wasn't like that. He'd said she was the first woman he'd touched in years. She'd believed him, and four years was a long time.

Aaron's thoughts were running along different lines. He felt he'd made a prize fool of himself. He should have remembered that Annabel had never shown she was interested in him in any shape or form. Why he was so obsessed with her he didn't know. He'd never sensed any warmth in her towards him, with the exception of when he'd had Lucy with him and during those moments when she'd been in his arms.

Apart from that she was cool, cold almost, and he doubted that it was only an unhappy childhood that was to blame for that. Annabel was right when she'd said she was nothing like Eloise. But if he married again he didn't want to be living with a carbon copy of his first wife.

He would want it to be a fresh start in every way and was constantly amazed that it had only been since he'd met her that he'd been thinking along those lines.

Let it rest, he told himself irritably as he undressed. You were living in a state of muted contentment before Annabel came. Revert back to that. But it was easier said than done with the memory of his mouth on hers and his loins aching at the contact.

The first-year children of a neighbouring primary school were waiting wide-eyed to be shown round the cheerful Rainbow and Lollipop wards.

The hospital had checked with the school to see if there were any parental objections and had discovered that apart from one nervous mother all the parents were in favour of the children being shown the inside of a hospital.

'I was in *there*,' Lucy was telling them, pointing proudly to the small side ward that led off Rainbow, 'after Dr Swain mended my head.'

Watching from a few feet away with one of the ward sisters by her side, Annabel hid a smile. She'd been right when she'd prophesied that this visit would give Lucy some standing amongst her classmates after her prolonged absence.

They were looking suitably impressed, some of them almost envious, and it was hard to keep a straight face. Aaron was to join them any moment. He was bidding farewell to Oliver who was going home after a very successful result from the brain operation. The convulsions had stopped. It was early days, of course, but the future looked good for him and his parents.

When Aaron joined them he was smiling and Annabel wasn't sure if it was because of his pleasure at seeing Oliver off in a much-improved condition or seeing his daughter and her friends waiting to be shown round, with their teacher in attendance.

Actually, his pleasure was a bit of both and, though she wasn't aware of it, her presence was adding to his happiness. Even though they hadn't exactly been best buddies since the night he'd called at the flat.

They had no problems with each other on the job. They were both too professional to let personal matters get in the way of their work with poorly children, though Annabel found herself wishing frequently that they were back on the old footing. But Aaron had given her an ultimatum. Plain speaking was required and she wasn't ready yet.

If *he* had any such thoughts he kept them well hidden behind a brisk air of competence and that was the present state of play. But now, seeing Annabel waiting for him with the children, he was reminded that this was *her* idea and concern for Lucy was at the heart of it.

She had a way with children. Lucy liked her and their young patients in the two paediatric wards reacted well to her calm air of reassurance. She would make a good mother, he'd thought a couple of times, and then had switched his thoughts elsewhere. There was no husband or children in the background so maybe Annabel wasn't that way inclined, having no experience of proper family life to fall back on.

They had both left themselves free for the next couple of hours, although each of them could be called away if an emergency arose. With Aaron leading the way, Annabel followed as they set off to tour the wards, operating theatres and the rest.

Aaron had had a warm greeting for the children's teacher. It had been plain to see that he and Nicola Edwards had a good parent-teacher relationship. She was a small, vivacious blonde, and it didn't escape Annabel's notice that she was a similar type to his late wife.

There was an odd little pain around her heart as she watched them walking side by side, leading the small crocodile of five-year-olds. Just how friendly were they? she wondered, and knew that the ache came from envy.

She wished that she herself was as easy in his company as Nicola Edwards. Instead of backing off like a nervous virgin as she had on that night when he'd shown her what real passion was.

But, of course, the curvy blonde teacher didn't have to work with Aaron. Didn't have to keep up a guard all the time because she was hurting and didn't want to have to tell him why.

Had Nicola ever been invited to dine with them? she wondered. Had Mary Lewis sounded her out as a replacement wife for her son? She certainly looked the part, compared to herself.

Lucy, who'd been at the front of the procession in her role as the star of the exercise, must have done some dawdling along the way as Annabel now found her beside her. As she smiled down at her, the little girl slipped her hand into hers.

'When are you coming to see us again, Dr Swain?' she wanted to know.

It was a good question. Annabel could hardly tell Lucy that an invitation wasn't likely to be forthcoming in the present climate.

'Soon, I hope.'

That seemed to satisfy Lucy and she had a change of subject ready.

'Uncle Richard was at our house last night and he was asking Daddy about you.'

'In what way?'

'I think he was hoping you might buy his house. I wish you would.'

'Why do you wish that, Lucy?' she asked softly.

'So I could come and stay with you.'

'But your daddy and grandma might feel lonely if you did that.'

'Grandma would be glad of the rest...and Daddy could take Miss out somewhere. She likes him, you know. Grandma says she reminds her of my mummy.'

'And what do you think?' Annabel questioned in the same gentle tone.

'I can't remember what Mummy looked like. I was only small when she went into the water.' Trusting blue eyes were looking up into hers and Annabel wondered what was coming next. 'Daddy was upset when Grandma said that, though I don't know why. What is a clone, Annabel?'

'It is something formed in the likeness of something else.'

Lucy frowned. 'I don't understand what that means either.'

Annabel smiled and gave her hand a squeeze.

'Don't worry about it, Lucy. It's grown-up talk.'

They were at the entrance to Rainbow Ward and as Annabel digested Lucy's comments she knew that the child wasn't the only one who wasn't sure what he'd meant. Whatever it was, his mother's comment hadn't been well received. Had he been irritated because she was still pursuing the 'finding him a wife' campaign? Or had he just been generally upset at the mention of Eloise?

He was watching her now, dark eyes unreadable, with the petite blonde teacher glowing beside him as the children filed into the ward and stood in a semi-circle.

There was no way his mother would ever liken herself to her daughter-in-law, Annabel thought wryly. Next to Nicola Edwards she felt six feet tall and droopy. The white coat covering a neat skirt and cotton blouse was only a shade paler than her complexion, and she had a sudden urge to run out and jump onto the nearest sunbed.

'So, Dr Swain, are we ready to meet the children of Rainbow Ward?' Aaron asked, and, bringing her thoughts back to why they were there, she managed a weak smile.

Laura, in the first bed, had been brought in the day before with a severe asthma attack, and though she was better today the eight-year-old looked tired and poorly, but she perked up when the children stopped by her bed and chatted happily to them.

Jessica, in the next bed, had just come up from Theatre after a tonsil operation and was still sleeping off the anaesthetic. Jamie, further along the ward, was happy to show off a leg in traction after a serious fracture.

There was an empty bed where Jack, the boy with ALD, had been. He'd been temporarily discharged until such a time that a bone-marrow donor could be found, but with the seriousness of the illness there was a strong possibility that he would be back before then.

Annabel looked across and caught Aaron's glance on her. He smiled and suddenly the curvy little teacher, the ward and the assortment of sick and well children became a blur.

She was in love with him, she thought as her heartbeat thundered in her ears. It wasn't just physical attraction or lust. She loved Aaron for what he was. Caring father, loving son, dedicated doctor. And if he never looked at her again she wouldn't forget how he had made her come alive.

But she was still the woman who'd slept with someone else's husband, albeit unknowingly.

There was a question in his eyes now and she realised that he must be puzzled by the intensity of her gaze. He wasn't to know that it was as if she was seeing him for the first time...

She'd been aware of his attractions and his dedication to the children in his care before, but now she was seeing him as the man she loved, and after the happenings of recent months it was as if a bright light had broken into her darkness.

'What's wrong?' he asked in a low voice above the heads of their small visitors.

'Nothing,' she mouthed back, and it would have been true if she could have taken him to one side and told him how much she cared for him, but there was something else he needed to know first and that was the problem.

The tour was over. Lucy's prestige was intact amongst her school friends and the children were being served light refreshments in the restaurant before their teacher took them back to school.

It seemed that they'd enjoyed the novelty of it and so had Nicola Edwards if her expression was anything to go by. But Annabel had a feeling that it was the doctor rather than his young patients that had put the smile on Nicola's face.

Within minutes of them leaving she was in Theatre and Aaron was preparing for his afternoon clinic. The visit from the school children had taken a slice out of their busy day and now they must make up for it.

In Annabel's case a child had been brought in with a suspected haematoma after a sign had fallen on him in a shopping mall. X-rays had shown that there was indeed bleeding inside the skull and surgery had been needed.

For Aaron the clinic was the usual run of sick and suffering children and when the door had closed behind the last one he let his thoughts go back to those moments on the ward.

He hadn't been able to take his eyes off Annabel. Why, he wasn't sure. Maybe it was because today had brought back memories of their first meeting and the circumstances of it. Or maybe it was just the case that every time he saw her it felt right.

He knew that Lucy's teacher was interested in him. They'd met on several occasions at school functions and when he'd suggested today's visit she'd been only too willing to fit it into the curriculum.

He knew what was in his mother's mind. She thought that Nicola's resemblance to Eloise might kindle some interest in him. So it looked as if she'd given up on Annabel, but *he* hadn't.

It was strange, almost as if her disinterested attitude was making him feel challenged. Yet he knew it wasn't that. He admired everything about her. Her acceptance of the solitariness that surrounded her. Her absorption in the job, and the way she was so good with Lucy. The only thing he wasn't too happy about was the way she was treating him.

Back there on the ward there'd been something in the atmosphere. He didn't know what, but she'd observed him with such a fixed stare that he'd felt as if she'd been trying to tell him something. But after the children and their teacher had gone and they'd had a moment to themselves, she'd had nothing to say, even though that same look had been there in her eyes.

He shook his head. Why after all this time did he have to be attracted to an enigma such as Annabel Swain? The little teacher was an uncomplicated soul. Why couldn't he fancy her instead of a leggy brunette, who was as closed as a clam when it came to what went on in *her* life?

But there were patients' notes to be written up from the clinic, various appointments for surgery to be made and a last round of the two wards before he went home. With Annabel in Theatre he doubted that he would see her again today.

But he was wrong about that. He hadn't been home long when the doorbell rang, and when he went to answer it she was on the doorstep, looking serious and uncomfortable.

'Can you spare a moment?' she asked as her heartbeat quickened at the sight of him.

'Of course. Come in. You look very solemn. Is something wrong?'

She was wearing a sheepskin jacket, tight-fitting beige trousers and soft leather boots to keep out winter's chill, and looked every inch the career-woman who was keeping him at bay.

'Is your mother in?' she asked in a low voice.

'No. She's gone to her bridge club. Why? Did you want to see her?'

She shook her head. 'No. It's you I came to see.'

'Really? Then let me take your coat.'

He sensed that she was feeling awkward and wondered what had brought her to his home. He was pretty sure that it wasn't as a follow-up to that night at her flat.

When Annabel was seated Aaron stood with his back to the fireplace, looking down at her, and when she didn't speak he said, 'So, to what do I owe the honour of your presence?'

The remark was meant to be jokey but she felt that there was sarcasm behind it.

'I've come to tell you something that was told to me

today,' she said levelly. 'I may be making too much of it, but I think it's something you ought to know. If I'm speaking out of turn, I hope you will forgive me.'

'You sound very mysterious. I'm all agog. What is it that you have to say?'

She wished she could say, I've come to tell you that I'm in love with you. Would he be 'agog' to hear that?

'A cardiac consultant from the Infirmary came to Barnaby's just after you left this evening. He's new and wanted to have a look at what we were offering in paediatric care. I take it that you didn't know he was coming.'

Aaron frowned. 'No, I didn't, otherwise I would have been there.'

'He remarked that his secretary left much to be desired, which I took to mean she'd forgotten to tell you he was coming. He said he would get back to you and only stayed a few minutes.'

Aaron still wasn't pleased. 'I take it that there is a purpose to what you're saying.'

'Yes,' she said quietly, wishing that there wasn't. 'The cardiologist said that he was looking forward to meeting you and that he'd had the pleasure of making your mother's acquaintance some weeks ago…at his room.

'You may already be aware of that and I'm making a nuisance of myself. But I thought that she might have some concerns about her health that could be at the root of her worries on your behalf. Obviously I didn't question him at all, and if I had I'm sure he would have reminded me about patient confidentiality.'

Aaron had been listening to what she was saying in amazement. It fitted in, he thought incredulously. Why hadn't his mother told *him* if she had health problems? And what were they.

A few weeks ago she'd complained of pain in her arms and general tiredness. So he'd employed a cleaner as well as the housekeeper who came in each day to assist.

He'd taken note that her colour was good and that she was eating well, and he hadn't made a fuss when she hadn't let him examine her, but this was something totally unexpected and it was no wonder that Annabel was embarrassed at having to point him towards what was under his nose.

'Did you know your mother was seeing a heart specialist?' she asked hesitantly.

'No. I didn't,' he said tersely. 'It explains why she's been trying to marry me off, bless her. She's thinking that if anything happens to her it won't be easy for me with the sort of job I've got and Lucy to care for. That's what my mother is like. Always putting Lucy and me before herself. Hence what she said to you and her comments about Lucy's teacher. I hope there aren't any more that I don't know about.'

'Yes. She must have felt she was scraping the bottom of the barrel when it came to me,' Annabel said drily.

He was observing her with the dark intent gaze that she was beginning to know so well as he said slowly, 'What do you mean?'

She laughed, but it was without amusement. 'Well, I'm not exactly a cuddly blonde, am I? I don't dress to kill, I live in a box of a flat and basically have very little going for me as regards the opposite sex.'

'Why are you putting yourself down like this?' he asked abruptly. 'Don't you ever look in the mirror? You've got good bone structure, wonderful eyes and legs that seem to go on for ever. And with regard to where you live, it's nothing to be ashamed of. I know I've gone on about it a bit, but it was only because I was concerned about you. I thought you deserved better and now you're doing something about it without any prompting from me.

'Regarding marriage, most women are married before they're thirty. You are different. You have a touch-me-not attitude that to someone with less determination than myself might be quite offputting. What happened between us the other night was an example. I'd no sooner touched you than you shied off. Surely you've had *some* experience with my sex.'

Aaron didn't understand, she thought bleakly. Her childhood had been blighted with the constant feeling of not being wanted and it had spilled over into adulthood.

'Yes, of course I have,' she told him stiffly. 'I dated guys when I was at college. But none of it was serious. I was more interested in my career.'

'And of late?'

'Of late I've had my fingers burnt. Shall we leave it at that?'

He sighed.

'Yes, if you say so. But, remember, if ever you need someone to talk to, I'm available. And now back to the reason for your visit. I'll speak to my mother when she gets in and take it from there. If there are problems of any kind in her life, I want to know. We have always helped each other through the bad times and this will be no different.'

His face was sombre in the softly lit room, and she ached to tell him that *she* wanted to share the bad times, too, if he would let her. But Aaron already had opinions about her lack of warmth and the last thing he would expect from her was the tenderness that was making her feel weak at the knees.

She turned to go. Having reluctantly butted into a private family matter, she'd done what she'd come to do, and now the polite thing was to depart and leave Aaron to his thoughts.

The next time she saw him she would know if her intervention had been warranted and she had a sinking feeling that she would find that it had.

'Thanks for taking the trouble to put me in the picture,' he said as he held her coat from behind while she pushed her arms into the sleeves. 'It couldn't have been easy being the bearer of such tidings.'

Her smile was rueful. 'It wasn't, but I had to make sure that you knew. Even if you thought me nosy and interfering.'

'Never would I think that of you,' he told her with a dry laugh, and as she swivelled to face him Annabel found herself in his arms.

'You can interfere in my life any time you want,' he said as their glances met, 'but when you do, make sure that it's what *you* want, too. Don't mess me about, Annabel.' And brushing her cheek with his lips, he pushed her gently towards the door.

Because she knew that it would all fall apart if she stayed, she went, out into the winter night, back to the life that was empty compared to his.

After he'd closed the door behind her Aaron went to stand by the window and watched Annabel drive away, but just outside the gate she stopped and he wondered why. Only to have the question answered when Richard from next door appeared at the side of her car.

He could see him in the light of the streetlamp, bending over to talk to her through the car window, which she'd wound down on seeing him. What was all that about? he wondered. Was Rick trying to push the sale of his house? Or had he other ideas in mind? It would be just like his friend the charmer to get through to Annabel where he couldn't.

Whatever the other man was up to, it didn't last long. Within minutes she was pulling away and Richard was going back into his own property. Aaron told himself he had other matters to concern himself with, more pressing than anything Richard was involved in. When his mother arrived home at just gone ten o'clock he was waiting for her.

'Yes. I have been to see a heart specialist,' she admitted when he told her about Annabel's visit. 'I had a word with our GP and told him I was having chest pains. He checked me over and recommended I see someone.'

'And why wasn't I informed?' he asked gently. 'It makes me look silly when you're involved with two members of the medical profession and I know nothing about it.'

'I didn't want to worry you. It's as simple as that. Remember, it's not so long ago that we nearly lost Lucy. I didn't want to put any more stress on you, Aaron.'

'And is that why you've been sounding out the unattached women of the parish?' he asked with a smile.

'It might have been.'

'And so what did the cardiologist have to say? That's the main thing.'

'He said that the strangling sort of chest pains I've been having were due to coronary artery spasm. Apparently my blood vessels narrow suddenly for a short period and then go back to normal. He also mentioned it can be connected with stress and both you and I had our share of that when Lucy was hurt. He has prescribed a nitrate drug to increase the flow of blood through the heart muscle and says that as long as I lose weight and avoid stress I should be all right. So, you see, I did the right thing in not worrying you.'

'No, you didn't. The verdict might have been much more serious and what would you have done then? Told me? Or still tried to keep it quiet? I'll have a word with the consultant when I see him, just to make sure there isn't anything else we need to know.'

Why was it that the women in his life didn't want him to know what ailed them? he thought when his mother had gone up to bed. Thanks to Annabel, he now knew what was wrong with her, but hc was no wiser regarding what the problem was with Annabel.

He felt instinctively that something had gone badly wrong in her life recently and understood if she didn't want to discuss it further. He would feel the same. After he'd lost Eloise he had no more been able to talk about the tragedy than fly. It had hurt too much.

But it didn't alter the fact that he would dearly like to know what was wrong with the woman who'd saved his daughter's life. What was it that was hurting her?

But he could be a patient man when something mattered as much as this. Just as long as Rick or someone like him didn't get to her first. He sensed that she was attracted to him, but there was no likelihood of Annabel rushing him to the altar, unlike the petite blonde school teacher, who'd done everything short of propositioning him while they'd been together that morning.

# CHAPTER FIVE

THE next morning Aaron sought Annabel out before his busy day got under way. He found her on her way to Theatre and she looked at him anxiously as he fell into step beside her.

'You were right about my mother,' he said. 'She *had* been to see the cardiac consultant at the Infirmary. I hadn't been told because she didn't want to worry me. Me! A doctor! Living in the same house and I didn't know she was seeing two others of my kind on a professional basis. Our GP and the heart specialist.'

The anxiety was still in her glance but there was relief in her voice as she said, 'So I didn't do wrong in telling you what I knew.'

'No. Of course not. I'm indebted to you, Annabel.'

'And your mother? Is *she* angry with me for butting into her private affairs?'

'No,' he repeated. 'She was dumbfounded when I faced her with it but is now relieved that I know what has been going on. The good news is that it could have been a lot more serious. The chest pains she's been having are apparently due to coronary artery spasms and the consultant has put her on a nitrate drug.'

'Thank goodness for that!' she breathed. 'That the problem isn't as serious as it might have been…and that I haven't done the wrong thing again.'

'I'm not with you.'

He watched the colour rise in her pale cheeks as she

replied, 'Well, I never seem to get it right when we're together.'

'You did once...for a short time. That night at your flat.'

They had reached the operating theatre and she was thankful that the clock above the door indicated that there was no more time to talk.

He smiled. 'I know. We both have a busy day ahead, but before we go our separate ways, I saw you talking to Richard last night. What did *he* want?'

He was butting into her private affairs yet again now, but he had to ask. His friend had only to smile and he had the women eating out of his hand.

'He saw me pulling out of your drive and thought he'd do a sales plug,' she said briefly.

'I see.'

He was only partly convinced but time was pressing and as he turned to go he said, 'How about lunch in the staff restaurant if we can make it coincide? There are a couple of things I'd like to discuss.'

'Possibly,' she said, her hazel eyes widening. 'But I'm not sure when I'll be free. We have a long list today.'

Aaron nodded.

'I know that. You always have. And I have an out-patients clinic that will be filling up at this moment. So we'll see how we go, eh?' And off he went.

Annabel had hardly slept after her visit to the Lewis house. Her thoughts had been dominated by the spectre of Aaron's mother being ill and herself being the one to make him aware of it.

But with the morning the outlook appeared brighter, especially if Aaron wanted her to lunch with him. Though with what she and the other surgeons had facing them, a lunchtime break might just be the dream it so often was.

So he'd seen her talking to his neighbour, she thought as she scrubbed up. He shouldn't have had to ask what they were discussing but he had. Aaron had warned her that Richard Clements had lots of women friends and it seemed as if he thought she might be willing to be charmed by him along with the rest.

If he did think that, he was mistaken. After her experience with Randy she would be able to spot a shallow type a mile off.

But this wasn't the time to be looking back. It was the future she was concerned with at that moment. Not her own, but the future of the little ones who would be receiving surgery in the hours to come. When minutes later she looked down on to her first patient of the day, a tiny baby with a serious congenital abnormality, all other thoughts were banished.

Shortly after birth the nursing staff had found little Phoebe to be frothy at the mouth, in need of frequent suctioning. The previous day they had tried to pass an orogastric tube to relieve the problem, but had been unsuccessful because of an obstruction in the oesophagus area. It had turned out to be a fistula and today Phoebe was to be operated on to remedy the problem. At the same time Annabel intended to make a gastrostomy so that feeding could commence.

It was a serious condition and surgery was imperative to prevent acidic gastric contents affecting the lungs. The baby had been seen by Aaron in his neonatal capacity and both he and Annabel were of the opinion that the condition would become life-threatening if not treated.

I couldn't do anything to save *my* baby, but I'm going to do my very best for you, little Phoebe, she silently promised the tiny red-faced infant, and from that moment everything but the needs of the child on the table ceased to exist.

Lunch had been and gone by the time Annabel was finished in Theatre and she resigned herself to having to wait to hear what Aaron had to say to her. He wasn't in his office when she went to seek him out and his secretary told her that he was chairing a meeting of community paediatricians about support for the families of children with serious illnesses.

'If you see Dr Lewis before I do, will you tell him that baby Phoebe came through the surgery all right and should soon be able to feed normally?' she told the secretary.

The middle-aged woman smiled.

'Yes, I'll do that. If that lovely wife of his hadn't died, I feel he would have had more children. I don't think he ever intended little Lucy to be an only child, but none of us know what life has in store for us, do we?'

Annabel nodded. She couldn't argue with that. But as she went off duty she was thinking that people like herself made their own grief while others had it thrust upon them. According to his secretary the departed Eloise had been 'lovely'. Obviously a hard act to follow!

When she got back to the flat there were flowers outside her door, cream roses. Just the sight of them brought tears to her eyes and she laid her head against the doorpost and howled when she read the card that was with them.

'Thanks again for taking the time to come to see me last night. It couldn't have been easy. Best regards. Aaron.'

It wasn't the words. They were brief and polite. It was

the thought behind them that was making her cry. She was in love with him, yet was afraid to show it in case she got a rebuff.

The thought had occurred a few times that she needn't tell him about the past.

And then there was the small matter of Aaron not returning her feelings. It was possible that *was* the case. Even though they had had one moment of magic in each other's arms, she'd spoilt it because of her guilt.

She sometimes thought that losing her baby had been a punishment, because she'd been stupid enough to assume that her relationship with Randolph had been strong and that he would be pleased if she conceived. A lot of women in an unmarried state would have been glad to be rid of such a responsibility, but no one could accuse her of those sorts of feelings.

After she'd had her meal, Annabel picked up the phone to thank Aaron for the flowers. A woman's voice answered and it wasn't his mother's.

'Could I speak to Aaron, please?' she said.

'I'm sorry,' the strange voice said. 'He only came in a few moments ago and is under the shower. Once he's changed we're leaving immediately for parents' night at his daughter's school. Can I give him a message?'

'No. I'll speak to him in the morning,' Annabel said, having recognised the voice at the other end of the line.

As she replaced the receiver she was thinking that it was carrying the parent-teacher business a bit far when he and Nicola Edwards were going to parents' night together. In his absence the woman was making herself at home in no uncertain terms.

Was she a regular visitor to Aaron's home? she wondered. They'd been chummy enough on the tour of the wards the previous morning.

So much for the new warmth that his flowers had kindled in her heart. They had been just a gesture. She'd been quick to make sure that any attraction he had for her was put into cold storage, and if he'd turned to a warmer creature than herself she had only one person to blame.

As he was knotting his tie in front of the mirror Aaron was wishing that he hadn't got himself embroiled with Lucy's teacher again, but a phone call to say how much she'd enjoyed the visit to the hospital *and* his company had been followed with the news that her car had developed a fault and could she possibly ask for a lift to parents' evening?

'I know you might be pushed for time,' Nicola had said, 'but I only live a short distance from you and could walk round to your place if that's all right.'

He'd said of course he would give her a lift, but had wished she hadn't asked. The signs were all there. He was being pursued and sooner or later he would have to give out signs that he wasn't interested in her.

His mother had gone to visit a friend and Nicola was chatting to Lucy when he went downstairs.

'Did I hear the phone?' he asked casually.

'Yes,' she replied. 'As the call came at an inconvenient moment I thought you wouldn't mind me answering it.'

'Not at all. Who was it?'

'She didn't say, but it sounded like Dr Swain. I asked if she wanted to leave a message but she said it would keep until tomorrow.'

Drat! he thought. Not only had he missed lunching with Annabel, he hadn't been there to take her call. Why was it that she always seemed out of reach while the woman passing on the message was beginning to seem forever under his feet.

'Are we ready, Daddy?' Lucy asked, and as he looked at his daughter his frustrations were blotted out in a rush of thankfulness. This night could so easily have meant nothing to him if Lucy hadn't been brought back to health and strength. If his relationship with Annabel never progressed any further, he would always bless her for that.

It was late when her doorbell rang and Annabel wasn't expecting it to be Aaron. Not after Nicola had told her that she and Aaron were going to Lucy's parents' evening together.

But it *was* him standing outside. He asked if she'd checked to see who it was before opening the door.

'Yes, of course,' she told him, as she stepped back to let him in. 'I never open up to anyone unless I can see who is out there. But the situation rarely arises as my visitors are few and far between.'

She was whingeing again, she thought as soon as the words were out. Why couldn't she greet Aaron with some sparkle just for once? But Miss Goldilocks had put the dampener on her earlier and he was the last person she'd been expecting to call round.

'I'm sorry I couldn't take your call when you rang earlier,' he said. 'I'd just got in and rushed upstairs for a shower. Nicola Edwards was keeping an eye on Lucy while I got ready as Mum was out, and it was she who answered.'

'Yes, I gathered that.'

'She had a problem with her car and rang to ask if I would give her a lift to the school and back. I've just dropped her off and Mum is putting Lucy to bed, so here I am.'

'I rang to thank you for the flowers.'

'I guessed that was it, but I still wanted a word with you and once we get bogged down at the hospital it isn't easy to find a spare moment. Like today, for instance. And talking about today, how did the little Phoebe come through the surgery?'

'Very well,' she told him. 'I asked your secretary to let you know but I presume you haven't been back there. I left Phoebe in Recovery and when she wakes up hopefully she'll be able to have her first proper feed.'

'That's good. I hate to see tiny babies in distress.'

Annabel could feel the familiar lump forming in her throat and turned away.

'What is it?' he asked. 'What's wrong?'

'Nothing,' she said, with tears glistening on her lashes. 'Just a moment of weakness.'

'Why, though? We see sick babies all the time.'

'Yes, I know we do.'

'So why are you so emotional over Phoebe?'

'It's not just Phoebe that I'm crying for.'

'I see.' And into the silence that followed he said, 'For someone who's never had a child herself, you have great compassion.'

She closed her eyes, trying to fight off the painful memories that were crowding back.

A voice was saying awkwardly in her mind, with the nasal drawl that she never wanted to hear again, 'I know I should've told ya, honey, but somehow the right moment never came. I have a wife and kids back home.'

Then later, much later, a gentler voice had penetrated her returning consciousness. 'I'm sorry, Annabel. We did our best, but you've lost the baby.'

She groped her way to a chair and sank down onto it. Aaron was by her side in a flash.

'For God's sake, Annabel. What is it? What's wrong?'

His arms were around her and she leaned her head weakly against his chest.

'It's nothing,' she croaked. 'Everything got on top of me for a moment. Probably because it's been a long day. I'm all right now.' And gently removing herself from his arms, she managed a smile. 'You must think me the most drab person you've ever met.'

'Drab!' he exclaimed. 'The workings of your mind are a mystery to me! You are a caring and competent surgeon who has a way with children and would make a wonderful mother, but when it comes to your private life you have no self-esteem.'

To be told that Aaron thought she would make a good mother brought the tears back again and as they streamed down her cheeks his expression changed from incomprehension to awareness.

'You want a child of your own. Is that it, Annabel? The ache inside you comes from that, and because you've been on your own for so long you can't cope with making that sort of commitment.'

'Yes, that's it,' she agreed, glad to be off the hook. At that moment the truth would have choked her in the telling.

Aaron was smiling. He couldn't help it. He'd solved the mystery. With patience and careful wooing it might all come right for them.

As she dried her eyes on the big white handkerchief he'd produced he said, 'So let's cheer up and talk about something else, shall we?'

She nodded.

'What are you doing over Christmas? It's only a few

weeks away and please don't start weeping again if it's looming emptily, as I'm not going to allow that.'

She managed a watery smile of her own. '*What* are you not going to allow? More tears or a lonely Christmas?'

'Both. You always seem to be doing things for me, while I've done nothing for you. As well as saving Lucy's life, you came to tell me about my mother, and for both those things I will always be grateful. So will you come and spend some time with us over Christmas?'

She was observing him with surprised hazel eyes. 'You're sorry for me, aren't you?'

'Concerned would be a better word.'

'What about the school teacher?'

'Nicola Edwards? What about her?'

'Wouldn't you rather have *her* presence over Christmas?'

'No. Why should I? She's just Lucy's teacher as far as I'm concerned.'

'I don't think she sees it like that.'

'Maybe, but that's her problem. I've never encouraged her.'

'Will your friend Richard be around?'

She watched his jawline tighten.

'Possibly. Do you want him to be?'

'Not particularly.'

'Right, then. So, what do you say? Will you join us, either to stay or have some meals with us, particularly on Christmas Day?'

'Whichever would be most convenient for you.'

'I'd like you to stay, so that you can see Lucy open her presents on Christmas morning.'

'That would be lovely,' she breathed.

'So it's settled, then.'

'Yes, it's settled.'

Not only would it be the first family Christmas she'd been part of in years, she would be spending it with the man she loved, and as her eyes brightened and her spirits lifted there was joy in her heart for the first time in many months.

'I'm going now,' Aaron was saying. 'For one thing it's very late and for another we both have a heavy day ahead of us tomorrow. But before I leave I want you to promise me there will be no more tears.'

'I promise,' she told him, and on that assurance he went.

As she lay waiting for sleep to come Annabel's thoughts were a mixture of happiness and dismay. The thought of spending Christmas with Aaron and his family was wonderful but she'd let him jump to the wrong conclusion. She'd taken the easy way out again, which wasn't in keeping with her normal behaviour.

Deceit was foreign to her nature. It was one of the reasons why she'd been so horrified to discover she'd been sleeping with someone else's husband, albeit unknowingly. But she accepted that, although Randy had deceived her, she wasn't without blame.

She'd told herself countless times that she should have checked on his background more thoroughly, and even more shamingly had asked herself if she had been guilty of using the man to get the child.

Now she'd met the love of her life and hadn't the courage to tell him that she'd misled him. That the ache inside her was for a child that she'd lost, not wishful thinking.

As Annabel walked the short distance from the flat to the hospital the next morning she was barely aware of winter's nip. Her mind was full of the Christmas to come and, having decided in her heart searchings of the previous night that she wasn't going to spoil it by telling Aaron about past indiscretions until it was over, she had a spring in her step that might not have been there otherwise.

A four-year-old boy with a serious congenital heart problem was first on the list for surgery. Charles Drury, who specialised in paediatric cardiology, was to operate, with herself to assist, and as they prepared for the operation Annabel felt that if ever there was an example of teamwork, this was it.

The child had been brought to the hospital's notice by a paediatrician working in the district who had been looking into a possible case of child neglect. When Aaron had seen him alarm bells had rung.

His mother had explained that he was often blue around the lips, fingernails and toes after even the smallest amount of exertion. He also spent a lot of time in a squatting position with his knees hunched up to his chest.

Aaron had passed him on to Charles Drury who had arranged an echocardiogram and tetralogy of Fallot had been diagnosed, a condition combining four heart defects—displacement of the aorta, narrowing of the pulmonary valve, a hole in the ventricular septum and thickening of the wall of the right ventricle.

These abnormalities meant that the blood pumped to the rest of the body from the heart was insufficiently oxygenated, hence the blueness of the child's extremities. It was a serious condition and if not corrected would drastically reduce his life span.

There was a risk. There always was in serious heart

defects in small children. But if anyone could correct the defects in the child's heart, Charles Drury could, and she would be there beside him.

It was over and the boy was in Intensive Care when she went to tell his parents that he'd come through the operation safely. She found his father pacing uncomfortably up and down the small anteroom where they had been waiting, while the mother was breast-feeding a new baby, with a toddler clinging to her skirts. Both of them were anxious to know when they could see him.

'You can see him now,' Annabel told them. 'But only for a moment. Your little boy will be in Intensive Care to begin with, then once we are satisfied with his condition he'll be put on the ward.'

At midday Annabel went for a quick bite. Aaron was in front of her in the queue in the staff restaurant.

Surprisingly he had Lucy with him, and when the little girl saw her she tugged at his sleeve and said, 'Annabel is behind us, Daddy.'

He swung round and as their glances met asked, 'Would you care to join us?'

'I'd love to,' she told him with a smile for Lucy.

When the three of them were seated Annabel asked, 'So, to what do we owe the pleasure of Lucy's company?'

'My mother is staying with an old friend overnight and when Lucy woke up with a sore throat this morning I didn't fancy sending her to school. I was expecting to leave her with the housekeeper who comes in daily but she rang in to say she'd had a family bereavement, so I had to bring her with me. She's been helping my secretary, haven't you?'

'And what about the sore throat?' Annabel asked. 'Is it any better?'

'Not much,' Lucy told her, and Aaron laughed.

'I think this young lady is enjoying bad health. She doesn't want to be bundled off to school for the afternoon.'

'It's not the ideal place for her, though, is it, if she's got a throat infection?' Annabel said. 'A hospital full of sick children.'

'Maybe not,' he agreed drily, 'but under the circumstances have you any other suggestions?'

'I might have.'

'Such as?'

'I've finished for the day. The two operations I had planned for this afternoon have been cancelled. The parents of the first child rang in this morning to say that he'd got a heavy cold and the second, a young girl due for a tonsillectomy, has moved house of all things without the family letting us know, and can't be contacted.'

'So?'

'I'll take Lucy back to your place and look after her until you've finished here.'

If Aaron had any doubts about the suggestion his daughter hadn't. Lucy clapped her hands and cried, 'Yes, please, Annabel. Can we play at doctors and patients?'

'We'll do whatever you like if your daddy says it's all right.'

'Yes, of course,' he agreed, 'but are you sure you want to spend the afternoon being bandaged from head to foot? I have no doubt about which of you will be the doctor.'

'I'll put up with it,' she said with a smile. 'Just as long as I don't have to take a dose of castor oil.'

'Or have an enema,' he remarked.

As their shared laughter washed over her Lucy asked, 'What is one of those?'

As Annabel put the key in the lock of the front door of Aaron's house it was a peculiar feeling. She was a stranger entering another woman's home. A home from which she was long gone. And beside her was Eloise's daughter, the enchanting Lucy.

It was a sensation that she hadn't experienced on her two previous visits, but on those occasions both Aaron and his mother had been present. Today it was different. She felt as if the house had been waiting for her, waiting for her to make her mark, but wasn't sure what was expected of her.

Did Eloise, wherever she might be, know that she was in love with her husband? she wondered. And if she did, did she approve? Would she be willing to allow Lucy into her safekeeping if ever Aaron told her he loved her as much as she loved him?

Without any such kind of thoughts plaguing *her* mind her small charge suggested, 'Shall we dress up, Annabel? If you don't want to play doctors and patients, we could be fairies. I have a fairy dress that Grandma bought me for my birthday and there's a dress of Mummy's in the wardrobe that you could wear. Daddy let's me play with it because it's all bright and shiny.'

'I don't think so,' she said quickly. '*You* can dress up for *me*, but I don't think your daddy would want me to touch what belonged to Mummy.'

'He won't mind.' Lucy persisted, lip trembling. 'Please, Annabel. Can't we be fairies for just a little while?'

Annabel looked at her in consternation. The last thing she wanted was for Aaron to find out that his daughter had been in tears while in her care. He wasn't due home for at least a couple of hours. Maybe there would be no harm as long as the garment was back in the wardrobe before that time.

'All right,' she agreed reluctantly, 'but only for a short time, Lucy. Where is the dress?'

'I'll show you,' she said, smiling now that her wish had been granted. Taking Annabel's hand, she led her up a wide staircase into the master bedroom. 'In there,' she said, pointing to a fitted wardrobe.

It was an evening dress of ivory silk with a beaded bodice and a full, flowing skirt. When Annabel tried it on the top half hung on her and the skirt was far too short, both factors a reminder that its owner had been more rounded and less tall than herself.

There was the faint smell of perfume lingering on the expensive fabric and she shivered. Was its owner watching her in the dress, indignant and helpless to protest? She felt as if any moment Eloise would appear and demand she take it off.

Lucy, meanwhile, unaware of Annabel's unease, was floating from room to room, waving her wand and enjoying herself immensely, when the door opened and Aaron was there, his face a study in amazed outrage and disbelief.

'What on earth is going on?' he demanded.

'We were playing at fairies,' she said hesitantly, as the bright colour stained her cheeks. 'Anything to keep Lucy happy.'

'Anything appears to be a good description,' he said in the same grim tone. 'Much as I love my daughter, I don't let her have all her own way.'

'Maybe. But what is someone like me to do when she is in tears? Let her become upset?' she protested. 'I want to get to know Lucy. She's a delightful child and I'd like us to be friends. It would have been a poor beginning if we didn't get on the first time we were alone together.'

He didn't comment. Instead, he told her stiffly, 'I came home to pick up some paperwork that I'd forgotten. How do you expect me to feel?'

'I'm sorry,' she croaked. 'I didn't mean to offend you. Lucy was upset when I refused to dress up for her, and rather than see her in tears I agreed. She said that you let her play with the dress so I thought it would be all right. I know it was taking liberties but the last thing I would ever want is to upset you, Aaron.'

'Yes, I do let Lucy play with the dress,' he admitted stonily, 'when she wants to feel near to Eloise...but really! The last thing I expected was to find *you* wearing it.'

In her dismay Annabel threw decorum to the winds. She undid the zip with frantic fingers and let the dress fall to the floor. When she stood before him in her underslip she didn't care that Aaron was seeing her undressed. All she wanted was to be free of the embarrassment.

Almost before he could take in the vision before him, she was reaching frantically for the skirt and blouse she'd been wearing previously and throwing them on as if he'd caught her naked.

He turned away, saying flatly, 'I have to get back. Are you free to stay with Lucy for a little while longer?'

She was calming down.

'Yes, if you're prepared to trust me.'

'*You* said that,' he reminded her in the same downbeat tone of voice, and departed.

*    *    *

Driving back to the hospital, Aaron was furious with himself. He'd just made a big song and dance about finding Annabel wearing the old evening dress that had belonged to Eloise.

She'd not been wearing it out of nosiness or insensitivity, but to please his child, and he'd read her the Riot Act. Anyone would have thought he'd caught her stealing the family heirlooms, such as they were, when instead she'd merely allowed Lucy to cajole her into something she hadn't wanted to do.

She'd given up her afternoon to do him a favour and he'd behaved as if she'd desecrated the memory of his dead wife, when instead she'd been looking after the living in the form of his daughter.

His annoyance had come from a source that Annabel was not aware of. He wanted his relationship with her to be separate in every way from the life he'd had with Eloise. If he'd wanted a clone of her he might have looked in the direction of Lucy's teacher, but he didn't.

He wanted the cool loner, with the hazel eyes, dark brown hair and slender coltish body, who once again was doing him a favour. All he'd done for her had been to act like a man who was still bound by the chains of the past.

His mouth twisted as he thought that after his outburst Annabel probably thought that he had no intention of ever replacing Eloise. And he'd put himself in a position where she wasn't likely to believe him if he told her the truth.

# CHAPTER SIX

WHEN he'd gone Annabel didn't know whether to laugh or cry. Yet knew she could do neither. Lucy was standing on one leg, waving her fairy wand limply and asking, 'Why was Daddy angry, Annabel? I play with the dress all the time.'

That may be true, Annabel thought wryly, but I don't. I overstepped the mark and now am back to where I was before Aaron entrusted me with his daughter. And if nothing else has come out of those embarrassing moments up in the bedroom, one thing is clear. Aaron hasn't let go of Eloise. I must have been insane to ever think he might turn in my direction.

But Lucy was waiting for an answer.

'He wasn't angry with *you*, Lucy,' she said with gentle reassurance. 'I think he was just a bit surprised when he saw me in your mother's dress.'

It was putting it mildly, but she didn't want Lucy to be upset by the incident, especially as it had been her idea.

For the rest of the afternoon they reverted to the original plan of doctors and patients, and when Annabel heard Aaron's car pull up outside some time later she was, as he'd prophesied, covered in bandages. She left Lucy playing in her room and went downstairs to meet Aaron.

'How's it gone, then?' he asked, as if their earlier confrontation had never been.

'Fine,' she said coolly, relieving herself of the bandages almost as quickly as she'd discarded the dress. She wanted to be off, back at the flat where she could think.

'I was unreasonable earlier,' he said flatly when she was ready to go. 'You took me by surprise.'

'Yes, I'm sure I did, and I'm sorry. You did me a favour, though, in spite of flying off the handle.'

He knew what was coming.

'You've made it very clear that, no matter what your mother or anyone else thinks, you're not ready to re-marry. I doubt that you ever will be.'

And as she made to leave she thought that if she stayed away from the child, which might be the sensible thing to do, there would be no doing the same with the father.

There was no way she could avoid Aaron. Not at Barnaby's anyway. But she could tell him that she'd had second thoughts about Christmas. He would get the mes-sage and who was to say he wouldn't be glad of a get-out after today's fiasco?

Every time she thought about him finding her in his wife's dress she cringed. Maybe she *had* been too eager to placate Lucy. Aaron had been quick to point out that she wasn't allowed all her own way.

But she was such a sweet child... and she didn't have a mother. No matter how kind and loving her grand-mother was, the child must feel it when she saw her friends with their mothers. The only person who could do something about that was her father, and after today the prospects didn't look good.

As she'd already decided, avoiding Aaron wasn't going to be easy while on duty, but she was going to give it a good try. Her face burned every time she thought about what a figure she must have cut in the dress with its too short skirt and too big bodice. And what he'd thought when she'd stripped to her underslip in her desperation to get it off, she didn't want to contemplate.

For any woman, undressing for the first time in front of the love of her life would be a special moment, but not for her...the queen of catastrophe. They'd had the bedroom scene all right, but it had been far from how she'd imagined it would be.

So it was a brief nod when they met on the wards or on the hospital corridors and if conversation was necessary regarding one of their small patients it was kept to the minimum.

To keep her mind occupied in her free time Annabel continued with her house-hunting, but it was with little enthusiasm and she knew why. She'd allowed herself to think that one day she would live with Aaron in the big, red-brick house that she so admired. Having come in from the cold at last, she'd thought that maybe, somehow, one day she would be part of a loving family for the first time in her life.

Now she was having to adjust and it was a painful process that was diminishing her desire to find a place of her own. She didn't want to be alone any more, she wanted to be with him. But it seemed that Aaron was content to live with his memories. It was as she'd thought all along. He just felt sorry for her.

As the shops, theatres, and restaurants were caught up in pre-Christmas fever Annabel wandered aimlessly around, hoping that it might wash off on her. But painfully clear in her mind was the moment when she'd told Aaron that she'd changed her plans and wouldn't be spending Christmas with him and his family. And after that there was little chance of her feeling in festive mood.

They'd spied each other in the hospital car park on a crisp winter morning and as he'd observed her doubtfully she'd taken a deep breath and gone to him.

'I won't be joining you for Christmas, Aaron,' she'd told him without preamble. 'I've made other plans.'

He'd sighed. 'What took you so long? I've been expecting to hear that ever since I found you in the dress. You say you have other plans. What are they? Christmas dinner for one in that dreadful flat?'

'That's my business.'

His face looked bleached in the light of a pale sun, but she told herself she wasn't going to weaken. She was a past mistress at bringing misery upon herself, and falling in love with Aaron was just another example of her poor judgement. Better this way than any more heartache. A clean break always healed more quickly than a compound fracture.

'I told you I was sorry,' he said, tight-lipped, 'but you're using what happened as a way out. It's given you an excuse not to join us. You're happy in your misery, aren't you, Annabel? That way you're safe.'

'That is good, coming from you!' she flung back at him. 'I thought we might have something, you and I, but *you're* the one who can't, or won't, let go of the past. Sometimes it takes an outsider like me to point out the obvious.'

His face darkened and she thought bleakly that between them they were only making things worse, so on a lighter note she said, 'We shouldn't let our differences affect Lucy. I'd like to buy her something for Christmas, if that's all right with you.'

'Yes, of course it's all right with me,' he said, still tight-faced. 'On one condition, though.'

'And what is that?'

'That you bring it round personally on Christmas morning…if it won't interfere with the other plans you've made. She'll be disappointed that you're not coming to stay, and it will make up for it a little if she sees you on the day.'

'You are trying to make me feel guilty, aren't you?' she said tonelessly. 'But, yes, I'll do that if you want me to.'

'It would appear that what *I* want doesn't come into it,' he replied with a similar lack of emotion, 'and as we've just about exhausted the topic, I'll be on my way.'

Reaching into the car for his briefcase, he pointed himself towards the hospital buildings, leaving her to make what she would of that.

So Annabel still thought he wasn't ready to move on, Aaron thought sombrely as he prepared to meet the day. He'd sent Eloise's clothes to various charities long ago, except for the dress which Lucy had begged him to keep so that she could use it for dressing up. And now Annabel was of the opinion that he had a morbid obsession with it.

He'd been hoping she wouldn't change her mind about Christmas, but her attitude ever since that day had made him think there was little chance of it, and she had proved him right.

Insisting that she bring Lucy's present personally on Christmas Day had been an attempt to coax her back into his family circle. Whether he would be able to persuade her to stay when she came was something he would have to wait to find out.

His mother had heard part of the story of the dress from Lucy and she'd said gently, 'It really *is* time to move on, Aaron.'

He'd made no reply, just nodded and thought sombrely that chance would be a fine thing. If ever there was a woman who wasn't falling over herself to get him to the altar, it was the hazel-eyed doctor who thought he was still mourning his wife.

He wished he knew more about her. She'd told him of her loveless childhood and that was all. When he was with her he was always conscious of melancholy within and sensed that it came from a much more recent source. But what that source was he had yet to find out.

It was a Saturday morning and Annabel was looking for inspiration in the town's biggest toy store when a voice said from behind, 'So we meet again.'

When she swivelled round Richard Clements was there, smiling his confident smile and observing her appreciatively. She smiled back, unimpressed. Annabel had no illusions about this man. He wasn't bowled over by her charms. Aaron's friend was the kind of man who would make the plainest of women feel attractive without too much effort on his part. But it was still nice to see a face she recognised amongst those of the jostling crowds.

'Shopping for the family?' he questioned.

'Not exactly,' she told him, with the realisation that if he had discussed her with Aaron, the man she loved had told him little about her. 'This is new to me. I'm looking for something for Lucy.'

He laughed.

'Me, too. So it's a case of well met. We can compare

notes and make sure that we don't both get her the same thing. Then maybe you'd care to join me for a coffee.'

Annabel nodded. He wasn't her type but he was company of sorts and was putting himself out to be pleasant, and by the time they'd made their choices, queued up and paid for them, a quiet coffee somewhere would be most acceptable.

'And so what have *you* got planned for Christmas,' Richard asked as they seated themselves in a nearby bistro with their packages. Annabel had bought Lucy a doll dressed as a fairy, hoping that Aaron wouldn't see anything significant in it, and the five-year-old would be receiving ice skates from Richard.

'Not a lot,' she told him evasively. 'I'm looking forward to a rest. Paediatric surgery takes its toll.'

'Hmm, I can imagine,' he agreed, sizing her up at the same time. 'Did you know that Aaron has been offered a job in Canada?'

'And is he going to take it?' she asked weakly.

'I don't know. *I* think he should go. Make a fresh start. Blow away the cobwebs.'

'But what about Lucy and his mother?'

'Well, obviously they would go, too.'

'Yes, of course.'

'Would you miss him?'

Was he kidding? She would miss all three of them, but Aaron most of all.

'Yes. I would. We work well together.'

'I wasn't meaning workwise.'

'I see. Yes, I would miss his friendship.'

'So you're not in line for the next Mrs Lewis?'

'That is for me to know and you to find out,' she said coolly, irritated by his questions.

'Sure,' he said smoothly, 'but Aaron is a great guy. I wouldn't want him to be given the run-around.'

Run-around! she thought angrily. That was good!

'I'm afraid that you've lost me,' she said, the chill in her voice increasing. 'Aaron is quite capable of fighting his own battles, I would imagine.' She got to her feet. 'If you'll excuse me, I must be off. I have a busy day ahead.' And before he could reply she was threading her way amongst the tables and chairs of the bistro and out into the crowds once more.

Busy day ahead! Annabel thought grimly as she drove back to the flat. Who was she trying to fool? And who had given Richard the right to question her about her private life? Certainly not her, or Aaron if the present state of affairs was anything to go by. He'd given up on her. She was sure of it.

But whatever dismal thoughts her meeting with Richard had conjured up, the news that Aaron might be going to live abroad stood out like the dark shadow of doom.

She hadn't known about the job offer, which wasn't surprising as they weren't communicating any more, but now that she did know she couldn't think of anything else. Surely Aaron wouldn't take his mother and Lucy to live in another land where they would know no one? On the other hand, they might view the prospect as something new and exciting.

'I met Annabel when I was out shopping this morning,' Richard told Aaron when he called round that afternoon. 'We were both shopping for Lucy.'

He had Aaron's attention immediately.

'You met Annabel?'

'Sure did.'

'And what did she have to say?'

Richard shrugged.

'Not a lot, but most of it was to the point.'

'Meaning?'

'I asked her if she was expecting to be the next Mrs Lewis and she froze on me.'

'Well, thanks for that!' Aaron exclaimed angrily. 'No wonder the chill set in. How could you ask such a personal question?'

'I did have your interests at heart.'

'It doesn't sound like it. The next time you're concerned about my interests, consult me first, will you? I've given Annabel cause to think I won't ever marry again, so she wouldn't be likely to take well to that line of questioning.'

'And are you sorry that you did?'

Aaron's mouth was tender.

'Yes, of course I am. You've seen her, haven't you? She's clever, beautiful, wonderful with children and straight as a die.'

'So why not do something about it?'

'I intend to, but your interference won't have helped. Annabel is the last person to be asking if she has hopes of marrying me. I can assure you that she has no plans for getting me to the altar. She is her own person and makes no pretence about it.'

'I thought from the way you speak of her that it was an accepted thing between the two of you that wedding bells might soon be ringing,' Richard said apologetically.

'Well, you were wrong,' Aaron told him. 'If *your* love life is thriving, mine isn't.'

'Yes, but I keep *my* affairs light. My life is a drifting sort of thing. With my job it wouldn't be easy to put down roots. But you are different, Aaron. And I may as well tell you, I have something else to confess.'

Aaron groaned. 'What is it?'

'I let slip about the Canada job.'

'And what did Annabel have to say about that?'

'Once again, not much.'

'I can imagine. You *are* the limit! I would rather have told her myself.'

'So are you considering it?'

'Maybe. Maybe not.'

'I think you should go. Get out of the rut you're in.'

'Do you really? I hardly think that bringing up my daughter, being there for my mother and holding down a demanding job is being in a rut.'

'Maybe not. But it doesn't fill that empty space in the bed each night, does it?'

'No. It doesn't. But unless it's Annabel who's going to be lying next to me, I'm not interested.'

'She's nothing like Eloise.'

'She doesn't have to be.' Aaron told him exasperatedly. 'I don't want a clone of my first wife. If I did, Lucy's school teacher would fit the bill.'

His friend was smiling again.

'Lucky you, having so many women in your life.'

'One, to be exact,' Aaron pointed out drily, 'and Annabel is now only on the fringe of it.'

On Monday morning Annabel asked Charles Drury, 'Did you know that Aaron has been offered a job in Canada, sir?'

The elderly consultant nodded. 'Yes. He mentioned it last thing on Friday night just as we were leaving.'

'Do you think he will take it?'

'It's a good opportunity. He would be perfect for it.

But whether he'll go, I don't know,' he told her. 'Personally I'm not in favour of the ''brain drain''. We need all the doctors we can get in this country. We're over-populated and understaffed.'

She'd discussed the possibility of Aaron moving with two people so far, Annabel thought as she went on her way, neither of them being the man himself, and really there was only he who could put her mind at rest…or shatter her dreams even more than they were already.

She decided that the thing to do was contrive a moment when they were in casual conversation and drop in a mention of the job offer. That way she might get to know his feelings on the matter without making an issue of it.

But there were no sightings of Aaron until just before midday, when his voice came from behind her as she was examining a small boy who had been admitted with a concussion from a blow to the head in the school playground.

'This child is from Lucy's school,' he said. 'Nicola is outside and most distressed about the accident.'

'Yes. I'm sure she must be,' she replied as they moved away from the bed. 'You can tell her we will be monitoring the child and unless any complications develop he will be allowed home as soon as we're happy about his condition.' And then added, unable to help herself. 'Is she the only teacher at that school? Or is it that she likes the hospital atmosphere?'

He pursed his lips. 'I think we both know that she is a caring teacher, and we are both aware that she is bent on getting to know me. Does that answer your question?'

'Maybe. But I have another one that I'd like an answer to,' she told him, knowing it was not going to be a moment when she could slip it into casual conversation. But she was going to ask it nevertheless.

'Yes?'

'I believe you've had a job offer from Canada.'

'Correct. Richard told you, didn't he?'

She nodded. 'Are you going to take it?'

There was nothing casual about that either, but she didn't care. She had to know.

'I've no idea. It only came up at the end of last week and there is a lot to consider before I make a decision.'

'Such as?'

She was cringing inwardly. It sounded more like the Spanish Inquisition she was putting him through than friendly curiosity.

He was observing her levelly and she met his glance with defiance.

'I know it's none of my business, but it will affect me from the job point of view if I have to get used to a new Head of Paediatrics.'

She was playing down her devastation at the implications of it by making out it was only the job she was concerned about, when the prospect of life without him was unbearable.

It was having the desired effect. Instead of telling Annabel that it all depended on her what he did with the rest of his life, Aaron said flatly, 'It would rest with how my mother felt about moving abroad. I can't leave her alone back here. I wasn't the only one who lost their loved ones that day in Cornwall. Mum would be desolate without us. As for Lucy, she's young enough to adapt to a new way of life without much trouble.' And then there's *you*, he wanted to tell her. More than anything there's *you*!

But he didn't because she was shrugging her shoulders and saying blandly, 'Yes, there *are* others to consider beside yourself, and don't be too sure that Lucy will settle in just like that. She's happy where she is. Children don't react well to change. It affects their feeling of security. That's my opinion anyway.'

Aaron's dark brows were drawn together as he said with dry sarcasm, 'And I suppose *you* would know, having had children of your own.'

As soon as the words were out he regretted them. It was a hurtful thing to have said. She worked with them, associated herself with them, even though she'd never been a parent.

But she was taking it all so calmly that he'd wanted to hit back, because he was miserable to the very fibres of his being at the gap that was widening between them with every second.

She'd turned away. Aaron had opened the wound again, she thought achingly. The mention of her childlessness had been like the pain of a knife thrust and she couldn't bear it any more.

'I lost a child shortly before I came to work here. I miscarried at four and a half months,' she said flatly, and watched his face stretch.

It was a bald statement of fact with no tears. She didn't want pity, just respect, and there wouldn't be much of that around if ever Aaron heard the full story.

'Ah! So that's the reason for your melancholy,' he said in slow surprise. 'Were you married, or was it an affair?'

'It was an affair that I felt could lead to marriage. But it fizzled out when I became pregnant.'

'You're saying that he left you to cope on your own?' he exclaimed incredulously.

'I wish I could have been there for you,' he said sombrely. 'Do you remember me asking if you'd been ill when we first met? You were skin and bone and so pale I wondered what was wrong. Well, now I know, and it explains some of the things that have puzzled me, though not all of them. How badly did you want a child, Annabel?'

'More than anything on earth.'

It was choking him to ask, but he had to. 'And the father. Who was he?'

She swallowed hard. 'Another paediatric surgeon. An American.'

'Where is he now?'

'Gone back to the States.'

'Are you in touch?'

'No. I've never spoken to him since the day I told him I was pregnant.'

What did you expect? Aaron was asking himself as his questions came pouring forth. A virgin? It would be too presumptuous to think that Annabel hadn't had some encounters with men.

'Did you love him?'

She shook her head. 'I thought I did, but those sorts of feelings soon disappeared when I saw how he felt about the baby.'

The fact that the man in question was already married had been the main reason for his lack of enthusiasm, but the words would stick in her throat if she tired to tell Aaron that.

They'd moved into the corridor while they'd been speaking and from there into a small garden beside the wards. And now as they faced each other amongst the dead leaves and bare branches of winter, there was a new warmth springing up between them.

She'd told him, Annabel was thinking, and Aaron

hadn't condemned her. But, then, he wouldn't because he didn't know the full facts. He'd been upset and concerned for her and it was like balm to her heart.

It didn't mean that things had changed in *his* life, but *hers* had certainly perked up. She touched him gently on the cheek.

'What?' he asked as his arms went round her.

'For being kind and not judging me.'

'No woman who is left to bring a child into the world on her own should be judged,' he said softly as he held her close. 'Nature is a fast mover when the sperm and the fertilised egg connect. But giving birth and bringing up a child is a lifetime commitment and is the hardest thing any woman is asked to do. Any man as well for that matter, but *he* doesn't have to suffer the birth pains.'

'A miscarriage isn't a bundle of laughs either,' she told him looking up into his dark gaze.

'What happened?'

'Nothing very unusual. I'd been called to Theatre in a hurry and was speeding along a hospital corridor that was still wet from cleaning. Down I went onto the hard tiles. Shortly afterwards I started bleeding and then everything went haywire.'

Aaron bent his head to hers and this time he planted a butterfly kiss on her mouth. As her lips parted at the contact urgency gripped him. He let out a groan. Why did they have to be on hospital premises? He wanted to take hold of this woman. Make love to her...if he hadn't forgotten how.

'What is it?' she asked, aware of his arousal.

'I want to make love to you, but it's hardly the place, is it?'

She laughed and Aaron found himself joining in.

'Hardly. Can you see the headlines, DOCTORS CAUGHT *IN FLAGRANTE* IN HOSPITAL GROUNDS.'

'So what are we going to do about it?' he asked with his voice deepening.

'Nothing,' she told him, reverting back to seriousness.

'Are you afraid that *I* might give you a child? Because I wouldn't, you know. I would never be so irresponsible. There is nothing more wonderful than a wanted pregnancy.'

He wasn't to know that having *his* child would be heaven on earth, she thought. But not if it meant another pregnancy where the father-to-be had his own agenda, and that was how it would be with Aaron. In his heart he still belonged to Eloise.

A porter was passing, pushing an empty trolley. When he saw them he gave a curious stare and Aaron let his hold fall away.

'So you don't want me to make love to you?' he said in a low voice.

'Yes. I do,' she told him, 'but not as a panacea or for easing of the loins. I've been down that road once, Aaron.' Two student nurses appeared in the wake of the porter. 'I think we need to go our separate ways.'

'I'll be in touch,' he promised, but she shook her head.

'Let's take it slowly.'

'All right. But what about Christmas? Are you going to change your mind?'

'I don't know. Can we talk about it another time? I see Nicola approaching.'

'Oh, no!' he groaned.

'Oh, yes,' she said.

It was to be a day to remember in more ways than one they found as the hours went by. A group of children from a day nursery had been admitted with suspected salmonellosis.

They were in various stages of distress from vomiting, diarrhoea and stomach cramps to a baby showing signs of septicaemia. In a short space of time all the paediatric beds were full and the waiting room crowded with anxious parents called from their daytime pursuits.

The children were arriving by the ambulance load, Annabel thought as emergency routines were put in place. The wailing of fretful children filled the air.

Rehydration therapy was being applied to those only mildly affected in the form of liquids only for twenty-four hours, while babies and children more poorly were receiving fluid replacement intravenously.

For baby Charlene there was deep concern. Both Aaron and Annabel had examined her and agreed that there were signs of blood poisoning. When the bacterium escaped into the blood, septicaemia could occur and the baby was in a serious condition.

She was alternating between high fever and chills, slipping in and out of consciousness, and was jaundiced. Glucose and antibiotics were immediately given intravenously and she was transferred to Intensive Care.

The source of the bacterium would be pinpointed by a culture grown in the laboratory but it would take time and in the interval the doctors would be on the alert for septic shock which could kill.

Meanwhile, the nursery would have been closed down and checked over by health inspectors. There seemed little doubt that it was the source of the infection and whether it had been caused by accident or negligence, there was trouble ahead for those running it.

Charlene's mother was a teenager, already overburdened with the responsibilities of motherhood and now rigid with fear on her baby's behalf.

'We are doing all we can to save Charlene,' Aaron told her gently as she wept by the cot. 'How long is it since she became ill?'

'She started last night,' the young mother sobbed. 'I was up with her all the time. This morning my mum said best take her to Casualty and they sent her here. It's that nursery, isn't it? I had to take her there because I have to work and so does my mum. Have you got kids?'

'Yes. I have,' he told her gravely. 'I have a daughter and she almost died not long ago.' His eyes were on Annabel, walking briskly down the ward towards them. 'So I know what you are going through. Why not go and have a cup of tea while Dr Swain and I take care of Charlene?'

'All right,' she agreed reluctantly. 'But you'll call me if she needs me, won't you?'

'Of course,' he agreed, and as Annabel joined him he said sombrely, 'It's not her mum this little one is going to need. She needs a miracle.'

# CHAPTER SEVEN

As THEY stood looking down on the baby Annabel's face was grave. She prayed there would be no need for amputation. But if gangrene developed in the extremities it might be the only way to save the infant's life.

It would depend on how quickly the antibiotics began to work and the results of the culture, as the medication might have to be changed according to what the bacterium was identified as.

Aaron was reading her thoughts.

'It's wait-and-see time,' he said soberly. 'I wouldn't want to wish that on you.'

'I've amputated before and will no doubt do it again if it saves a child's life,' she said with equal seriousness, 'but never on such a small one. How old is she? Ten? Eleven weeks?'

The mother was back and they dredged up smiles. No point in putting that horrendous burden onto her young shoulders yet, Annabel thought. It would be time enough if it turned out that they hadn't managed to halt the blood poisoning.

That night she couldn't sleep. She'd told the night staff to call her if there was any worsening of the baby's condition, and she found herself listening for the sound of her bleeper.

Added to her concern and a cause for sleeplessness on its own merits were those moments with Aaron in the hospital garden. He'd been tender and caring and she'd started to hope again.

The influx of sick children had pushed the memory of it to the back of her mind, but now it was there again, clear and comforting, and as her thoughts wrestled between anxiety and pleasure the night wore on.

In his bed in the house at the other side of town Aaron was doing no better. As he tossed and turned in a half-doze he was dreaming about telling the young mother what they were going to have to do to save her baby, and every time he flung his arm across the empty space beside him the picture changed and Annabel was there, holding out her arms and smiling.

At two o'clock he'd had enough. Padding into Lucy's room he looked down at his daughter sleeping peacefully and sent up a prayer of thanks. Then, seeing a crack of light coming from under his mother's bedroom door, he tapped gently and went in.

She was reading, as he'd expected her to be. A poor sleeper, she often whiled away the night hours with a book.

'What is it?' she asked, peering at him over the top of her glasses.

'I'm popping out for a while,' he told her. 'I want to check on the baby I was telling you about.'

She nodded. 'I was expecting it.'

As Annabel pulled on trousers and sweater and reached for her warm sheepskin jacket, she was telling herself she was crazy. There had been no call from the night staff. No emergency with regard to Charlene. Yet she still couldn't settle.

It was only a short walk from the flat to the main hospital entrance and as she strode out into the night she looked up. Snow was falling, soft, white and fast. A reminder that Aaron was waiting to hear if she'd changed her mind about sharing Christmas with them.

A silver moon was lighting the pathways and gardens surrounding the hospital and her heartbeat quickened. It was a magical sight, the soft flakes falling to earth beneath its rays and not a soul in sight—until the main entrance came into view and then it was a different picture. Ambulances coming and going. People moving around. Reminders that illness and accidents were not just events of the day.

When she reached Intensive Care she saw a tall figure bending over Charlene's cot in the shadowed ward and her step slowed. It was either a staff member, an intruder, the baby's absent father or, as he turned at the sound of her footsteps, someone else who'd found sleep hard to come by.

'What are *you* doing here?' Aaron asked softly.

'The same as you, I imagine. I couldn't sleep and thought I'd pop across to check on the baby.'

'She's going to make it, I think,' he said, his voice lifting. 'Her fever is subsiding. I've been having nightmares about telling that young mother of hers we would have to amputate. Thank goodness she's improving.'

'Where is her mother?'

'Dozing in the waiting room next door. The poor kid is exhausted.'

'No father on the scene yet?'

'No. Probably some macho man teenager. Old enough to make her pregnant but lacking the maturity to face up to his responsibilities.'

She'd known someone like that herself, Annabel thought, not ready to face up to his responsibilities, and *he* wasn't a teenager. But she didn't want depressing thoughts intruding into this moment. Charlene wasn't out of danger yet, but she was certainly better and, taking his hand in hers, she said, 'Let's go and tell her mum.'

They had a cup of tea with the night nurses and chatted for a while then, after checking on the baby again, they made their way outside into the enchanted night.

'I'll walk you home,' he said, 'and come back for my car when I've seen you safely inside.'

She didn't argue. For once they were in harmony. Tired as she was, she didn't want the night to end. The snow was still falling steadily and bending to scoop up a handful she found that Aaron had had the same idea. As she tossed it at him he was ready for her and that started it. For the next half-hour they pelted each other until, glowing from the exertion, they collapsed outside the flats.

'Are you coming in?' she gasped.

He'd seen the invitation in her eyes and said laughingly, 'Don't tempt me. Although I do have an excuse for stripping off… I'm soaked to the skin. But I've never indulged in casual sex, Annabel, and it's the last thing I'd want with you.'

He was getting to his feet and brushing the snow off, and she desperately wanted him to stay. But he'd just cut her down to size, hadn't he? Hinting that, whatever *she* did in her relationships, *he* had his standards. And that was with him only knowing part of her situation.

'I'll see you shortly,' he called over his shoulder as he trudged off. 'It's five o'clock already and I might have to dig the car out.'

It was three days later and most of the children suffering from the salmonella outbreak had gone home. The culture had confirmed that the bacterium had come from a dairy product and once the source had been identified normal routine had been restored at the nursery, although not all the children had gone back as some parents had lost confidence in it.

Charlene was progressing well and all the staff were delighted to see her getting better, including the two doctors who had paid her a nocturnal visit and ended up wet and breathless in the snow.

'How's Lucy liking the snow?' Annabel asked one day, when she and Aaron had a moment to spare.

'She loves it, needless to say,' he said with a smile. 'Like someone else I know. My mother couldn't understand where all my wet clothes had come from the next morning. I hope it lasts until Christmas. And talking of Christmas, are you going to change your mind? It's the time of year when Lucy misses her mother most, I miss my wife the most and my mother misses my dad the most. Having you with us would make all the difference.'

Annabel was observing him in surprise. 'So you didn't invite me because I was a lost soul?'

'Of course not. Admittedly, I didn't want to think of you being alone, but it was for our sakes too that I asked you to stay with us.'

'Well, I might be able to fill the mother spot if Lucy will let me. The wife vacancy I don't think exists as far as you are concerned, and I don't think your mother would want me to wear a shirt and tie to fill the gap your father left. But if you really want me, I'll come. I'm sorry to have messed you about.'

'That's great,' he said quietly. 'And maybe over Christmas we'll get the chance to discuss the ''wife vacancy'', as you describe it.'

*     *     *

She'd bought Aaron a piece of amethyst crystal for Christmas. It was his birth stone and as she'd wrapped the beautiful shard that time and nature had created, she'd never felt more alive.

She had chosen it with loving care, taking no heed of the cost. Her wish was to please him, to give him something that he would cherish as part of the exciting present instead of the sad past.

Because in recent days, ever since they'd frolicked in the snow, the present *had* become exciting and full of promise. It had been a mistake to think Aaron was obsessed with what was gone. Annabel could feel it in her bones that they were back on track.

In a week it would be Christmas and now she had no doubts about where she wanted to be during that time. Expecting it to be a non-event, she'd volunteered to be on call over the holiday and there was no way she would want to change that, but hopefully she might not be needed and if she was, she would be with the one person who would understand.

There was just one blot on the horizon. Christmas with Aaron and his family was due to start with a party on Christmas Eve. She would move in with them in the afternoon and stay until the day after Boxing Day. But on the day before that he sought her out and, observing her apologetically, said, 'I thought I'd better mention that my mother has invited Nicola to tomorrow night's party. She felt that we owe her for the interest she's taken in Lucy and for her concern when the accident happened, and of course we do.'

In her new-found happiness Annabel smiled.

'So what? It's your house, your party, I don't mind who you invite as long as you are there.'

His expression cleared and he said with a smile of his own, 'You can depend on that.'

But when he'd gone it hadn't stopped her from wishing that Nicola hadn't been invited, with her cloying, coquettish ways.

In keeping with the new purpose in her life, Annabel had bought lots of new clothes—evening wear, day wear and lingerie. As she packed a small case on the afternoon of Christmas Eve, there was colour in her cheeks and a sparkle in her eyes.

The suit of smooth cream wool she'd chosen to wear until it was time for the party clung to the soft curves that had come back with her new vitality, and she hoped that Aaron would notice.

Mary opened the door to her, with Lucy hovering by her side, and if there had been any chill left in her heart their welcome would have taken it away.

'Come in my dear,' Mary said as she hugged her to her and Lucy grabbed her hand and pulled her inside.

'Aaron won't be a moment,' his mother said. 'He's been at the hospital all morning and is upstairs getting changed. He tells me that you're on call over the holiday. It's a pity that Mark Lafferty couldn't fill the slot. He has no family commitments like the others.'

'I *did* volunteer,' Annabel reminded her, 'and I also have no family commitments.'

Mary laughed.

'We'll have to see what we can do about that, then, won't we?' And the two women exchanged companionable smiles.

When Aaron came out of the bathroom Annabel was

across the landing, unpacking her case and generally settling into the guest room.

As he padded across the landing draped in a towel he
saw her through the open door and stopped.

'So you've arrived,' he said buoyantly. 'Did Mum tell
you I've only just got back from the hospital?'

She nodded. 'Problems?'

'Aren't there always? But they're sorted. Christmas is
upon us and you look beautiful. If I wasn't all damp I
would follow that comment up physically, but I don't
think you'd want your suit wet, would you?'

She laughed, still on a high, and said teasingly, 'I
could take it off.'

He pushed the door to behind him with his foot and,
following her lead, said, 'If you'd like to lean forward I
could manage a kiss without wetting you.'

Bending from the waist with lips protruding, she
obliged. But not for long.

Lucy was calling up the stairs, 'Grandma says she's
made a pot of tea, Annabel.' Aaron had to make a swift
departure.

It was going to be wonderful, she thought as she
looked down at his wet footprints on the carpet. She was
so happy she could burst.


'Wow!' he exclaimed when she came down the wide
staircase that evening in a strapless dress of pale gold
that clung to her waist and swirled around her ankles. It
made her hair and eyes look like soft brown driftwood
and the tilt of her mouth had an invitation all of its own.

She was lovely, this clever, dedicated doctor, he
thought tenderly. The time really *had* come to move on
with his life and if she would agree to be part of it his
happiness would be complete.

'Will I do?' she asked in a low voice.

*'Will you do?'* he echoed.

Taking her hand, he took her to where mistletoe hung in a bunch above the doorway and kissed her soundly, while behind them Lucy clapped her hands in excited approval.

There were some of Mary's friends at the party, including an ex-army officer with whom she seemed to be on very good terms. Richard was there with a svelte auburn-haired woman by his side…and Nicola, who surprisingly seemed to be lacking her usual effervescence.

Charles Drury and his pleasant grey-haired wife were holding court in a corner of the sitting room and Mark Lafferty ambled in during the course of the evening and told Annabel that she was a fine woman, a comment that made her think he had been imbibing the wine.

She was enjoying herself immensely. Every time her glance met Aaron it was there, the promise of what was to come, and her sparkle increased.

Over supper Annabel found Nicola by her side and the petite school teacher said disconsolately, 'I can see where Aaron's affections lie and it isn't with me. I hope you'll both be very happy.'

It was an awkward moment and Annabel didn't know what to say. She was sorry for the other woman and admired her generosity of spirit, but it was a bit early for congratulations so she gave her a sympathetic hug and said nothing.

When all the guests had gone and Mary had said a fond farewell to her ex-major before going up to bed, Aaron and Annabel were clearing up after the party.

'Do you think that my mother has been coaxing me into finding a new wife because she's ready to fly the nest herself?' he asked as they filled black refuse sacks.

'It's possible, I suppose,' she replied, her colour deepening. 'She and Thomas Parbold did seem very fond of each other.'

'He's from the bridge club that she goes to every week,' he explained. 'I've heard her mention him, but tonight was the first time we'd met.'

'What did you think of him?'

'He seemed very nice. Smartly dressed, straight as a ramrod. Not always the case with men of his age. I liked him. But do I fancy him as a stepfather?' he said quizzically. 'He was an officer in the army and I don't want to have to stand to attention every time he's around.'

'What would happen if you went to live in Canada? Would he sweep your mother off her feet and persuade her not to go, do you think?'

'Canada!' he echoed blankly. 'I'd forgotten about that. It's been the last thing on my mind in recent days. When you asked me about the job offer the other day I wanted to tell you then that it would depend on *you* more than anyone whether I accepted it. But it wasn't the right moment.' He'd dropped the bag of rubbish and was moving towards her.

'You know I'm in love with you, don't you, Annabel? Have been from the moment we met, when I kept wanting to put you on some vitamins. I've discovered since that beneath your frail exterior is an amazing woman.

'I *have* let go of Eloise, you know. I'm truly sorry about that business with the dress. You are very different from her in every way, and that is how I want it to be. You are your own person and so was she. So am I for that matter, and at this moment I am asking if you would take us on, Lucy and I. I love you and so does Lucy.'

'You shouldn't need to ask,' she said softly. 'After what has happened to me during the last twelve months

I thought I would never be happy again, but you've changed all that, Aaron.'

He held out his arms and she went into them. As the clock struck midnight he said softly, 'Merry Christmas, Annabel. May it be the first of many that we spend together. As for Canada, there's plenty of time to discuss that.'

It was Christmas morning and it seemed as if they'd hardly gone to their beds before Lucy was calling. 'He's been! Santa Claus has been!' And on a more awed note she added, 'He's eaten the mince pie and drank the sherry we left him.'

Standing tousled and bleary-eyed in their dressing-gowns, Annabel and Aaron showed themselves to be suitably impressed and settled back to watch Lucy open her gifts.

Every moment of the holiday had been enchanted so far, Annabel was thinking. Not least when they'd been clearing up the night before and Aaron had told her he loved her. Nothing could equal the joy of that. And as the day progressed, with Christmas dinner in the late afternoon and a walk afterwards in the snow which was still persisting, her happiness was unabated.

When Lucy had gone to bed that night they were alone. Aaron's mother had gone to a party at the major's house with the same crowd who'd been there the night before, and the little girl, over-excited and tired, had eventually dropped off to sleep.

Seated together on the sofa in front of a crackling log fire, Aaron was holding her close, stroking her hair and kissing the smooth cheek nearest to him, when the phone rang.

'Damn!' he said. 'Who can that be?' He glanced at

the contented figure beside him. 'I hope it isn't the hospital for you.'

It wasn't. She didn't know who it was but could tell that it wasn't anyone from Barnaby's, although there was consternation in his expression.

'When did this happen?' he asked sombrely.

'Last night! Christmas Eve! How could he be so cruel? Yes, of course I'll come. Don't concern yourself about Lucy. I have a friend staying with me. She'll be there if she wakes up.'

When he'd replaced the receiver he stood for a moment with a furrowed brow, then turned to Annabel and said, 'That was Terry Sullivan's wife, Magda. You know, Terry, my deputy.'

'Yes, I know him,' she agreed, wondering what was coming next as the call had obviously been about some sort of emergency.

'He's been having an affair with one of the sisters at Barnaby's and she's pregnant. That item of news was his Christmas present to Magda and the children last night. They were invited to the party but didn't turn up and now I know why. The poor woman is in a terrible state. Completely demoralised.'

'And where is *he*?' she croaked as the all too familiar story line unfolded.

'Terry's still there. For how long I don't know. But he won't want to leave his kids. The philandering rat! And as for women who steal the husbands of others, often because they can't get a man of their own, they are the lowest of the low.'

In his indignation Aaron hadn't seen her colour drain away or the horror cloud her eyes. He was leaning over and saying gently, 'I have to go, Annabel. I know it's ruined our evening but that poor woman needs someone and I'm fond of Magda and the boys. Terry can stew as far as I'm concerned, but I have to be there for them. What a Christmas they must be having!' Unaware that he had just blighted hers, he went, calling over his shoulder, 'If you're called out, ring me and I'll come straight back.'

She wasn't called out. Would have felt better if she had been. There would have been no time to talk when he came back. No time to tell Aaron the full story about her past stupidity.

His face was grim when he returned a couple of hours later.

'What a mess!' he hissed. 'Magda is on the verge of collapse and the children are trying to grasp what's happened without really being told the full story. As for Terry and his bit on the side, I would imagine that they're both wishing they'd never bothered.'

'So he's staying with his family, is he?'

'Yes. If Magda will let him. But how she's going to cope with watching another woman carry his child, I really don't know.'

'Which of the ward sisters is it?' she asked.

Not that it mattered. She was merely prolonging the moment, but her face stretched when he said, 'I don't know her name but she's tall, with brown hair and eyes like you.'

It was as if her heart had stopped beating. So the villain of the piece looked like herself. Very fitting.

'The man who fathered *my* baby was married, Aaron,' she said tonelessly. '*He* had a wife and family. That was why he wasn't over the moon when I told him I was pregnant.'

His face became even whiter than hers.

'I don't believe it! You had an affair with someone

else's husband. So you only told me half a tale. Thought that the seedy part of the story was best left unsaid.'

'Yes, but it wasn't how you think,' she pleaded.

'Don't make matters worse by making excuses,' he thundered.

After that she went upstairs and packed her case without a word from him and let herself out of the house like a thief in the night, and that was probably what he saw her as. Someone who had stolen his trust, his confidence and was well and truly back on the sidelines.

Back at the flat Annabel stood tearless and drained in its small hallway. She'd had two days of supreme contentment and should have known it wouldn't last. Why did she have to give her heart to a man as moral as Aaron Lewis? A man who saw no grey, just black and white. Yet his integrity was one of the things she loved most about him.

If he'd given her the chance to tell him that she hadn't known Randy had been married Aaron might have calmed down, but he hadn't wanted to know. She'd condemned herself out of her own mouth and not been given the chance to explain the true circumstances.

She had to make him see that he wasn't the only one who didn't sleep around. She hadn't exactly fallen into bed with him at the first opportunity. If she was guilty of anything it was taking Randy at face value. Being a trusting fool and not looking into his background.

Aaron's castigation of her had hurt. It had been totally unjust and in the midst of her devastation anger was kindling.

She'd already paid for her affair with the American with the loss of her self-esteem and the much more painful loss of her child. And now she was being made to pay again.

Well! Once was enough. Aaron could continue to wallow in self-righteousness. And while he was at it he could go to Canada, and see if *she* cared...

But, of course, she did care. She cared so much that the rest of the holiday was a blur of tears and angry avowals.

She was called out on Boxing Day, having to put aside her misery to cope with the problems of others.

A child had been transferred to Barnaby's with injuries from a road accident. The parents had been driving home in a winter dawn after an all-night party when a drunken driver had swerved into their vehicle. The father was in Intensive Care at the Infirmary with multiple injuries, the mother had escaped with cuts and shock and their six-year-old son was unconscious with injuries similar to those Lucy had sustained when she'd fallen off the climbing frame.

Annabel had never felt less like performing a tricky operation, especially one with such personal connotations, but she had no choice. A child's life was at stake and that was what she was there for. To save it if at all possible.

Her own problems belonged to that other life where she was the woman who didn't come up to scratch. But there in the operating theatre she was going to rise above all that, God willing, and use her expertise once again for the good of a child.

When Mary Lewis came home in the early hours of Boxing Day she found Aaron gazing sombrely into the dying embers of the fire.

'Annabel gone to bed?' she asked casually.

He shook his head.

'Then where?'

'She's gone,' he said heavily.

'Gone! Gone where?'

'Back to her place.'

'But why?'

'I had a phone call from Magda Sullivan earlier. She was in a terrible state. Terry's been having an affair with one of the nurses and she's pregnant. Needless to say, Magda isn't coping. Apparently he told her last night. Christmas Eve. What a start to Christmas, eh?'

His mother sank down onto the nearest chair.

'What a start indeed,' she agreed. 'But what has it got to do with Annabel?'

'It appears that she was involved in a similar situation at the hospital where she worked before.'

'What? She had an affair with a married man?'

'Exactly. *And* she fell pregnant.'

'And where is the child now?'

'She lost it.'

'Poor Annabel.'

'That was what I thought when she told me. But I didn't know the full story until tonight.'

'And now that you do, your feelings have changed?'

'Yes. No. I don't know how I feel. One thing is for sure. She won't come back after what I said to her. Why couldn't she have been honest with me?'

'Maybe she thought that it had nothing to do with anyone else. That it was her business, and hers alone.'

'That's all very well. But I more or less asked her to marry me. However, after seeing the state of Magda and her children tonight, witnessing the devastation that kind of thing can cause, I have no time for men who cheat on their wives or women who covet the husbands of others.'

'So it's over, your relationship with Annabel?'

'What else would you expect?'

'I don't know. I really don't know. But from what I've seen of her, Annabel doesn't strike me as the sort of person who would willingly hurt anyone.'

'Well, she's hurt me and will have hurt Lucy when she finds out that her wonderful Dr Swain isn't in our lives any more.'

'And are you bothered about the degree of Annabel's hurt in all this?'

'Of course I am. As a doctor I have the greatest respect for her—'

'But as a woman you're not so sure?'

He was on his feet. 'I'm not sure about anything any more.' Planting a kiss on her worried brow, he said, 'I'm off to bed. Maybe when I've slept on it I'll see things differently.'

# CHAPTER EIGHT

As THE new year approached, with its promise of new beginnings, Annabel accepted there would be none for her. In harness again at Barnaby's after the Christmas break, she and Aaron were back to being polite strangers, still bound by their commitment to the children there, but otherwise experiencing the bitter taste of an aborted love affair that had shown him to be relentless and her sparing with the truth.

Annabel had heard nothing from Mary and had concluded that she was now just as low in her esteem as she was in her son's, until they met one day in the town.

Both women had gone to the sales. It was Annabel's day off and, dreading the long hours with nothing but her thoughts to occupy her, she'd gone to make a lukewarm foray around the stores.

So had Aaron's mother, but there'd been nothing half-hearted about Mary's shopping spree. Her friendship with Tom Parbold was flourishing and for that reason, like any other woman with a new man in her life, she felt she needed new clothes.

The two women met in the self-service restaurant of one of the stores where Mary spied Annabel seated at a table by the window, gazing into space with her meal untouched.

'May I join you, Annabel?' she asked, as the young doctor observed her in surprise. Without waiting for permission, she unloaded the contents of her tray onto the table and settled herself opposite.

Annabel managed a smile. She had no quarrel with this pleasant woman. Had no quarrel with her son for that matter. It was Aaron who had put an end to their relationship.

'I've been wanting to talk to you ever since Christmas,' Mary was saying, 'but I wasn't sure how you would feel about us having a chat. I don't want to intrude into your life, Annabel, but I have a miserable son at home and a bewildered granddaughter and would like to see them happy again. Aaron has told me some of what happened between you and I can see both points of view. Sadly he can't. He'd put you on a pedestal and…'

'I fell off,' Annabel replied with a smile as wintry as the day outside.

'Do you want to tell me about it?' the other woman coaxed gently. 'You might feel better if you did.'

'There's not much to tell. I had an affair with another paediatric surgeon. He was an American, and a charmer. I didn't mean to get pregnant, but as I've always wanted a child of my own I had no problem when I did. I thought he wouldn't have one either. But when I told him about the baby he confessed that he was already married to someone back in the States. I immediately ended the affair as husband-stealing is not in my line, but decided that I was going to have the baby no matter what. As you will know, I lost it and, desperate for a new start, I came to work at Barnaby's.'

'So you didn't know that this man was married?'

'No. He deceived me. But I feel that I was equally to blame for taking him at face value.'

Mary sighed. 'That is the problem. Those of us who

tell the truth expect the same of others, and it doesn't always work out that way. But, tell me, why didn't you explain to Aaron that you were unaware of this man's circumstances?'

'I tried to, but he wouldn't listen.'

As Mary observed the shadows beneath her eyes and the defeated droop of her mouth, she ached for both her son and the woman he loved. She had no doubt that Aaron still loved his clever doctor, and if the state of Annabel was anything to go by, her feelings hadn't changed either.

'I understood his anger and disgust,' Annabel went on. 'He'd just come back from the Sullivan house and seen what distress that kind of infidelity can cause. And I must have had a death wish as I chose that moment to confess. I'd wanted to tell him right from the beginning, but dreaded what would happen. But when Aaron was caught up in a similar situation I felt that I had to tell him, even though I knew what the consequences would be. And I wasn't wrong.'

'So let me tell Aaron that you didn't know the American was married.'

Annabel shook her head. 'No! Please, don't. If Aaron can't accept me for what I am, there is no point in taking it any further. Promise me that you won't say anything.'

Mary sighed again.

'This is all so sad. But I won't say anything to Aaron if that is what you want. Though it's hard to stand by and do nothing when I might be able to put matters right.'

'The only person who can put matters right is Aaron,' Annabel told her bleakly, 'and something tells me that will be a long time in coming. But enough of the woes of foolish people like he and I. Tell me about Lucy. How is she? Having been banished from her life, I'm really going to miss her.'

It had been a gruelling day at the hospital. A packed clinic in the morning, with ward rounds in the afternoon, and for extra measure there'd been staff shortages for Aaron to cope with in the aftermath of Christmas.

And the day hadn't gone down any better, with Annabel not being around. When she was there they were polite strangers and when she wasn't he ached for the sight of her.

When he got home Lucy was waiting for him, and after playing with her while his mother put the finishing touches to the meal, he'd gone into his study and sat staring at the amethyst crystal. It was brittle and beautiful like the woman who'd given it to him, he thought. Annabel had to be hard to do what she'd done to him.

Yet he'd seen her with Lucy and the children in their care. Witnessed her pain at the loss of her own child. So why had she given so little thought to what might hurt *him*?

When his mother called out that dinner was ready he got to his feet, hoping that he might manage a pretence of an appetite, but food was the last thing on his mind when she said casually, 'I had lunch with Annabel today.'

Before he could comment Lucy asked, 'When is she coming to see us again, Grandma?'

'I don't know, Lucy,' she said. 'You'd better ask Daddy.'

'What did she have to say?' he asked, letting that pass.

'Not a lot. As she's feeling hurt and angry she didn't send her love, if that's what you mean. But, then, you would know that isn't likely to happen as you must bump into each other all the time at Barnaby's.'

His smile was grim. 'Am I to take it that I'm being told off in a roundabout sort of way?'

His mother's face was solemn. 'Just talk to her, Aaron. That's all I ask.'

When Lucy had gone to bed he waited until she was asleep and then reached for his coat and car keys.

'I won't be long,' he said, and his mother nodded, hoping that her words had sunk in.

When he got to the flats there was a red Porsche parked outside and his eyes widened as he saw the number plate. It was Richard's car. His jaw tightened. What was *he* doing here?

At that moment they came out. Annabel and Richard. He saw that her sparkle wasn't missing now. He was holding her arm and she was laughing up at him. Jealousy rose in him, raw and painful.

So much for that, then, he thought grimly as they got into Richard's car and drove off. Maybe he hadn't been wrong after all if Annabel could get over her broken heart as quickly as that.

The car was outside the coach house when he got back, and when he looked through the study window he could see their shadows on the blind, close together, intimate.

He had his answer. Annabel was attracted to men like Richard. The philandering type. He might not be married but he was always on the lookout for female company. When she compared the two of them *he* must seem like a judgmental bore.

'You're soon back!' his mother exclaimed disappointedly.

'Annabel is next door with Richard,' he told her. 'They were just leaving the flats when I got there.'

She sighed. 'I see.'

The next morning they met once again in the hospital staff car park and when Annabel would have walked past Aaron called, 'Have you got a minute?'

'Yes. What do you want?' she asked, knowing that by now his mother would have told him they'd met in town.

'It would seem that you are very resilient. That you soon bounce from one relationship to the next.'

'What?' she exclaimed, her wide hazel gaze fixed on him. 'You've lost me, I'm afraid.'

'Richard Clements.'

'What about him?'

'I saw him at the flats and then he took you to his place.'

'So?'

'I thought he wasn't your type.'

'He isn't. Richard rang me in the late afternoon, trying to persuade me to give his house a second viewing. I told him that I didn't think you would want me to live next door to you and that it would be too big for me in any case, but he coaxed me into having just one more look. I still wasn't interested and he brought me back before going to some club in town. Sorry to disappoint you.'

She was turning away, shoulders drooping in her big winter coat, and he wanted to tell her he was sorry, that he loved her, and could they start afresh? But she was off, eager to put as much distance as possible between them. Having no wish to make a further nuisance of himself, he followed at a much slower pace.

When she'd calmed down it occurred to Annabel that she hadn't asked Aaron what he'd been doing outside her flat. Had he been coming to see her by any chance and walked into the Richard scenario?

And what if he had? They were finished. He'd made that crystal clear and if Aaron thought she was going to beg he was very much mistaken.

The mother of the small boy that she'd operated on after the car crash on Boxing Day was waiting for her when she arrived at the wards. He was due to be discharged soon after making a good recovery from the skull fracture, and his father was now out of Intensive Care at the Infirmary.

She was holding a bouquet of flowers and said, 'Our family will soon be reunited back home, but before we are I just wanted to say thank you, Dr Swain. You gave up part of your Christmas to save our boy and we are truly grateful.'

Aaron appeared at a leisurely pace just as the boy's mother was making for his bedside and caught Annabel fighting back tears.

'What's wrong?' he asked, as the tenderness she always aroused in him blotted out every other emotion.

'It's just the kind thought that's getting to me, that's all,' she choked. 'Finding that not everyone thinks I'm rubbish.'

His face paled. 'I don't think that.'

'Yes, you do. You've made it very clear.'

'Tell me something,' he said levelly, 'do you think you treated me fairly? Only telling me half the story of what happened with this other man.'

She shook her head. 'No. I don't. But there was a reason. I knew how you would react and I certainly wasn't wrong about that.'

'I adored you, thought you were the most wonderful thing to happen to me since losing Eloise.'

'And you found me to be a sham?'

'Not a sham. A disappointment.'

The tears were still hovering on her lashes as she told him. 'I admired you from the moment we met. Your integrity, your love for your family, your strength of character. And yet it's those things that turned you against me. So from now on I'm staying how I was before, on my own. It's easier that way.'

Taking the flowers into the staffroom, she put them in water and then prepared to meet the day, not caring whether Aaron was still standing where she'd left him or turning cartwheels down the ward.

It was New Year's Eve, the time each year when the hospital held its staff Christmas party. And when Aaron heard Annabel tell Mark that she was thinking of giving it a miss, he said quickly, 'The trust expects the doctors to support the event, either alone or with our wives, husbands or partners.'

'So are you saying that I have to go?' she asked coolly.

'No, of course not. What you do outside working hours is your own business, but most of us do make the effort.'

It was only partly true. Most of the staff did attend, mainly because it was a prestigious affair, but the hospital trust didn't take particular note of who was there. It was he who wanted her to be present. He didn't want her to be on her own on the night that took out the old year and brought in the new.

It must have worked as minutes later she said stiffly, 'Then I suppose I'd better attend. Never let it be said that I've offended someone.'

He ignored that and went on his way, satisfied that

she would be visible to him that night, even if she wasn't in his arms. Though they might dance together if Annabel wouldn't think she was being patronised. And as for the rest of it, when it came to midnight, what then?

She still made his heart leap and his pulses quicken every time he saw her. If she came in the gold dress that she'd worn on Christmas Eve, the ache in him would be unbearable.

When they'd exchanged presents on Christmas morning and Lucy had found her doll, his mother the cashmere shawl that Annabel had bought her and himself the amethyst, he'd given her a gift-wrapped box of his own, holding a necklace of emeralds and diamonds.

'It's beautiful, Aaron,' she'd said huskily, 'and will be perfect with the dress I intend to wear for the party tonight.'

It *had* been perfect with the gold dress and now he wondered if he would ever again see her wear his first gift to her.

The snow had gone and it was a clear cold night as those staff not on duty filed into the conference room which had been changed into a party venue for the occasion.

The men were in evening dress and the women attired accordingly. Needless to say, Aaron stood out among his companions and there were some present who thought that he had it all—except for a woman in his life.

There had been rumours on the hospital grapevine that he and the new surgeon had something going, but there were no obvious signs of it so far. Looking just as impressive as he, she'd turned up in a long black dress that showed off her smooth shoulders and the rise of her breasts beneath a plunging neckline, but Annabel was keeping a low profile.

She was glad that she'd come. This was better than letting in the New Year on her own, but she wished that it could have been without the constraint between Aaron and herself. The moment midnight struck she would be off. Away from all the frustrated hopes and dreams that lay in fragments around her.

During the meal Annabel had Mark on one side of her and a young physiotherapist on the other, and as she watched him exchange languishing glances with one of the nurses she thought wryly that their love affair, at least, seemed to be on track.

Aaron was seated directly opposite her, which made it difficult to avoid his direct, dark gaze. Every time she looked up it was on her, but it wasn't giving any clue to his thoughts.

Maybe he was expecting her to make a play for someone before the night was out and was surmising who it was going to be, she thought. It would be in keeping with his opinion of her. He would have a surprise if it turned out to be him.

If she used her new-found attractions to light the fire between them again and then disappeared at midnight like the pantomime heroine, would he come the next day to seek her out? She doubted it.

There was a small dance floor at the other end of the room and when the meal was over those present seated themselves around it or disappeared into the bar.

After allowing Mark to lumber round the floor with her in an ungainly waltz, and following it with a much more skilful rock and roll with a young porter, she was beginning to enjoy herself.

Aaron was deep in conversation with the head of the hospital trust and she was free to watch him unobserved.

Until he turned suddenly and with a farewell shake of his superior's hand moved to her side.

When he spoke it was the last thing she was expecting him to say. 'I thought you might have been wearing the gold dress—and the necklace.'

'And what is that supposed to mean?' she asked coolly. 'That you don't approve of what I *am* wearing?'

'No. Of course not. It's just that you looked so lovely in it.'

'Really. But aren't you forgetting that was before I was cast aside? Maybe I don't want to be reminded of that time. And as for the necklace, you will be receiving it back shortly in the post. It's already packed and waiting to be sent off.'

'I don't want it back. It was a gift.'

'So was my love. But you didn't think twice about throwing it back at me, did you?'

He took her hand and raised her to her feet. 'Let's dance, before we have an audience. We're not here to entertain other people with our affairs.'

She eyed him mutinously, making no move towards the dance floor, and he said in a low voice, 'Either you dance with me, or I pick you up and carry you out.'

Both prospects were appealing but she wasn't going to let Aaron see that. Instead, she conceded regally, 'I'll dance with you, if you insist.'

When his arms went round her Annabel closed her eyes. This was the medicine she needed, but without the bitter aftertaste. Because there would be one, of that she had no doubt.

Their steps matched perfectly, she thought. Their bodies were moulded together as if they were one, but it was in their minds that the fault lay. She had paid the price of a bad error of judgement, twice over. So why was Aaron so determined she should pay a third time?

It was heaven to have Annabel in his arms again, Aaron thought, even though it was only for a matter of minutes.

He was a fool to have hurt her like he had. But his angry incredulity hadn't diminished. Had she thought so little of him that she couldn't tell him the truth? he'd asked himself countless times.

His mother had suggested that she probably hadn't known the man had been married. But how careless could one be? To give one's affections and loyalty to someone whose background was unknown.

He knew she loved children, wanted babies of her own, and was desolate that she'd lost a child. He would have given her babies. He loved them as much as she did. But now the chances of that were nil as long as they stayed in the limbo of disapproval.

The music was dying away and the dancers returning to their seats, but he didn't loosen his hold.

'I want to talk to you somewhere private,' he said quietly.

She wasn't encouraging. 'What about?'

'Us.'

'There's nothing to say.'

'I don't agree. If you won't come outside, I'll say it in front of everyone.'

'You're making a lot of threats,' she said laughingly, 'but as you are being so demanding, I'll do as you ask.'

'We'll go into my office,' he said. 'We shouldn't be disturbed there.'

'Tell me something,' Annabel said when they'd closed the door behind them a little later, 'what is it that's so urgent tonight, when we've been around each other workwise ever since Christmas?'

'I have something to tell you that I only found out today. My mother wants to get married again, to Thomas.'

Her face lit up. 'That's wonderful.'

'Yes, it is,' he agreed with a quirky smile. 'I'm really happy for her. Tom Parbold is a good man who will make her happy. The only fly in the ointment is that she's refusing to commit herself because of Lucy. She's concerned about who will look after her while I'm working and won't name a date. Then there's the Canada job, but I've told her that I'm not going. All that I care about is here.'

Her heart had warmed to hear that, but Annabel was listening to him in perplexity.

'Is this leading somewhere, Aaron?'

'Yes. Can I tell her that our romance is back on and we're going to get married, so that she'll start making her own plans with an easy mind?'

There was silence in the room as what he was asking of her sank in.

'That's rich, coming from someone who can't stand people who don't tell the truth,' she said in a voice that she barely recognised as her own.

'Yes, but it's in a good cause.'

'For whom?'

'My mother, of course. She deserves some happiness before it's too late.'

'And how is she going to feel when she finds out it isn't true?'

'She'll be married to Tom by then, and I will sort something at my end that is safe and secure for Lucy.'

'Why not ask Nicola to be your stand-in wife? She

would jump at the chance, especially if there was a view to permanency.'

'Because I prefer to ask you.'

Her heart was racing but she shrugged her shoulders and said casually, 'It's nice to know I'm useful for something. I'll do it. But it will be for your mother's sake, not yours.'

'Thanks, Annabel,' he said sombrely. 'I don't expect any favours from you. Maybe I don't deserve them. I don't know. But I appreciate you agreeing to fall in with the idea.'

'And what is going to happen once your mother and Tom are married? Do we stage a quarrel? It shouldn't be difficult.'

She watched him flinch.

'We'll worry about that when the time comes,' he said levelly. 'Is it all right if I tell her tomorrow?'

'Of course. What better way to start the New Year than with a falsehood?'

'Look, Annabel, if you don't want to do it, say so now.'

She'd already decided that it was better to be a pretend wife than none at all.

'I've said I'll do it and I will. But remember that it's just a charade.'

His eyes had been on her mouth and the swift rise and fall of her breasts in the low-cut dress, but he let his hands fall away at that and said, 'All right. You can make the rules as long as I call the shots.'

'And the first of those is to be?'

'That you come to the house tomorrow and we tell her then. Mum won't believe it if you aren't there.'

'And after that?'

'It should be easy enough to convince her that we're still madly in love.'

'And how will we do that?'

'Like this,' he said, taking hold of her again. His mouth came down on to hers, caressingly, bone-meltingly.

For the first few moments Annabel gave herself up to pleasure of it, but then she drew away from him. It would be so easy to accept this play-acting and the perks that went with it, but if Aaron thought she was going to be succumbing in his arms at frequent intervals and then discarded like an old shoe once the wedding was over, he had another think coming.

'I've just reminded you that it's a charade you're planning. No need to start practising beforehand. That sort of thing doesn't come into the curriculum when your mother isn't around.'

'Then we'd better get back to the party,' he said, unperturbed, and went to open the door.

For the remainder of the evening they mixed with the rest of the staff and gave no inclination that on the following day an engagement would be announced. When 'Auld Lang Syne' was sung they were on opposite sides of the room, and the first person to wish her a happy new year with a lingering kiss was the porter that Annabel had danced with.

When it was Aaron's turn he smiled. 'So I'm allowed *this*, am I? You don't see it as part of the charade?' He kissed her gently this time and when he released her said in a low voice, 'You won't have to suffer me for long. Once Mum is happy about us, her wedding will only be a matter of weeks.'

So he really was just using her, Annabel thought as she undressed in the cramped bedroom of the flat. She was involved in a farce that sprang from Aaron's love for his mother. The fact that he was involving her seemed to bother him little, as he intended that she would be dispensed with for a second time once Mary was married.

He'd made it quite clear so she had no excuse to feel used. Yet that was what he was doing, using her, and like a fool she was going to allow it, because she was fond of Aaron's mother. She also adored his daughter and, much as she understood him not wanting to interfere in his mother's happiness, she wanted to make certain that Lucy wasn't going to suffer if her grandmother got married.

The obvious way to make sure of that was to carry the plot through to its conclusion. For herself to be there always for the little girl. If it was as a wife in name only, it would be as a *mother* in every sense of the word.

The idea might appeal to Aaron as he'd made it clear that he saw her as being there to be used, and it would be an ideal arrangement for Lucy because they were already very fond of each other. But it wouldn't be good for herself. Not good at all, being in his life and yet not counting.

But nothing might come of any of it—that was her last thought as she drifted into sleep. She couldn't see Mary believing that Aaron and herself had resolved their differences so quickly. And a false engagement would be like walking on eggshells in front of all those that knew them.

She was to discover that she'd been mistaken about that. When she arrived at Aaron's house on New Year's Day his mother greeted her with open arms and kissed her soundly when she opened the door to her.

'This is wonderful news, Annabel,' she said. 'Especially for Lucy. You will be so good for her. She loves you already.'

'Thank you,' she croaked guiltily. 'It's very nice of you to say so. I believe that you also have congratulations due. I do hope that you and Tom will be very happy.'

'I know that we will.' She beamed.

This is awful, Annabel was thinking. How dare Aaron ask me to be involved in this? It has to stop immediately. Where is he?

As if reading her thoughts, his mother said, 'Aaron is upstairs. You'll find him in Lucy's room.'

She went up the stairs two at a time. Voices were coming from Lucy's play room and when she stood on the threshold they were there, father and daughter, snuggled together in one of the chairs while he listened to her reading from one of her school books.

Annabel's resolve was weakening. He was doing it for those he loved, she thought chokingly. Doing what he thought was best for his mother and Lucy. If what was best for *her* didn't come into it, too bad.

'Hello, there,' she said, and imagined that his eyes lit up when he saw her.

He put Lucy gently to one side, got to his feet and came towards her.

'How long have you been here?' he asked, hugging her to him.

'Just a few minutes, but long enough to know that your mum is happy about us,' she said with false heartiness.

'Yes. Tom is on his way over at this moment and they're going to sort out a wedding date. He's bought a very nice apartment on the strength of Mum saying yes and now all they have to do is get married.'

'Isn't it exciting, Grandma getting married?' Lucy cried.

'It certainly is,' he said buoyantly, and Annabel eyed him stonily from within the circle of his arms.

# CHAPTER NINE

WHAT Aaron had said to Annabel the night before, when he'd persuaded her to leave the party for the privacy of his office, had been basically true. His mother *had* refused to set a date for marrying Tom Parbold because of her concerns for Lucy and, because he loved them both dearly and would never do anything to upset either of them, he had been keen to find a solution to the problem.

But he also loved Annabel more than he could ever have imagined and had regretted the hurt he'd caused her. Somehow he'd had to put things right but hadn't thought that going down on his knees would have much effect in the circumstances.

He'd added one or two embellishments of his own in persuading her to fall in with his plans, but had kept the main reason for them to himself. He wanted her back, desperately, just as he wanted his mother to be happy and Lucy properly looked after.

There was no way he intended having his daughter fobbed off onto a succession of childminders. The only person he wanted to care for Lucy besides himself was Annabel, and he was hoping that by the time his mother's wedding day dawned he would be forgiven and the future would be theirs.

When she'd agreed to participate he'd felt a great knot of uncertainty begin to unwind. But there were tricky days ahead and she'd reminded him in no uncertain terms that what they were doing was a pretence, when all the time he wanted it to be real.

For the rest of the day they played the parts of lovers reunited and every time he kissed her or even touched her Annabel had to remind herself that it was a game they were playing.

She was still not sure how she was going to cope in the weeks to come. Would she be able to endure Aaron's attentions during that time, knowing them to be a very convincing act, when she craved for the sincerity of what they'd had before?

But she'd agreed. She'd put her hand to the plough and couldn't turn back in the face of Mary's happiness. Yet if she found that Lucy's life was to be less than secure once her grandmother had left the family home, she would have much to say to Aaron and a lot of it he wouldn't like.

When she was ready to leave for home he came out onto the drive with her. Taking advantage of the fact that they were alone for the first time since she'd arrived, Annabel said, 'In all the excitement of weddings and sham engagements, have you definitely turned down the Canada job?'

'Yes. They've been on to me again, but I told them I hadn't changed my mind. Maybe some time in the future but not now,' he said.

He didn't tell her that the only thing that mattered at the moment was themselves. He had to put matters right between them and he wouldn't be able to do that if he was in Canada.

With that thought in mind he had her swivelling round to face him in surprise as she was about to get into her car when he said, 'Don't send the necklace back, Annabel. I want you to keep it. And with jewellery in mind, I think we should go shopping tomorrow to put the final touch to the performance we're putting on for my mother.'

'What do you mean?'

'A ring. An engagement ring.'

'Are you serious?' she asked angrily. 'For what we're doing, a rubber band would be sufficient.'

He *was* serious. To have Annabel with his ring on her finger, no matter what the circumstances, would be one step nearer to putting right the mess he'd made, but it was to be expected that she wouldn't see it that way.

'Humour me in just this one thing,' he said.

'All right,' she agreed. 'Though I don't see the sense in it. I'll hang onto the necklace and return it along with the ring when the charade is over.'

She thought that might have got to him, pierced his infuriating complacency, but he just smiled and said, 'Time enough to concern yourself about that when the occasion arises.' And with a quick squeeze of her hand he let her go.

They chose a ring in the afternoon of the next day. It was a hurried affair, the last thing Annabel would have wanted it to be if it had been for real. But as it wasn't it didn't matter that they made a rushed visit to a jeweller's when they had a few minutes to spare.

'Have you any preference?' Aaron asked as they looked around the display units.

'Oh, yes. I've got lots of them,' she told him. 'I would prefer not to be mixed up in your scheming, worthy though it is. I would prefer not to have to wear a ring. I would prefer—'

'You've made your point,' he said in a low voice, 'so can we please do what we are here for? Do you like diamonds? Rubies? Or emeralds like those in the necklace?'

'I'd like a ring with a single pearl,' she told him. 'They say that pearls are for tears. I've shed mine, but there could be others coming when your mother finds out there won't be any wedding bells for us and Lucy's life is turned upside down.'

The words were no sooner out than she wanted to take them back. She'd let him see the depth of her hurt. Pride should have stopped her from doing that.

As he'd listened to her she'd seen Aaron's calm desert him for the first time since he'd asked her to help him convince his mother that their romance was alive and flourishing.

'If *I've* made you cry, I'm sorry, Annabel,' he said as a dark flush suffused his neck. 'You've had enough things to cry about in your life without me causing you grief.'

He wanted to tell her that he was hoping that it would all end in joy rather than tears and that to see his ring on her finger would be a part of it. But she was checking the time and saying flatly, 'Let's just pick the ring, shall we? I'm due in Theatre in half an hour.'

He nodded. Their thought processes were so far apart they might as well have been living on separate planets.

When they'd left the shop, leaving behind a shop assistant who was thinking that they'd been the least in love couple he'd ever served, Aaron said, 'What are you doing tonight?'

'Nothing.'

'Would you like me to put the ring on your finger now, or somewhere more atmospheric?'

'Now will do,' she told him. 'No point in making an even bigger farce of what we're doing.'

Annabel was thinking that she needed to get away from him before the tears she'd referred to came back in floods, and as he did as she'd asked she looked down bleakly at the milky perfection of a single pearl set in a delicate band of gold. It was a beautiful thing, the ring that was to tell everyone they belonged together. What a pity that it was just a prop for the pantomime.

Charles Drury was the first person they saw when they got back to Barnaby's. He'd just finished his rounds on the two main wards and was making his way back to his office.

When Aaron told him their news he smiled. 'So the rumours that have been going round weren't rumours after all. Congratulations to you both. My wife and I have had thirty-five happy years together and I hope it will be the same for you.'

Aaron was watching Annabel's expression out of the corner of his eye and he thought wryly that she was probably thinking that thirty-five weeks, or even days, would be nearer the mark where they were concerned.

Charles went on to say, 'You have a fine man here, Dr Swain. Kind, caring, excellent at the job. I'm sure he'll take those qualities with him into your married life.'

Aaron was squirming. The last thing Annabel needed in the present climate was a description of his worthiness. But he couldn't fault her. She was looking up at him fondly and murmuring, 'I'm sure that you're right, sir.' If there was mockery in her glance when it met his, he had only himself to blame.

'This really is a day for good news,' Charles said as he observed them with benign approval. 'Young Jack with the ALD is back with us.'

'Oh, no!' Annabel exclaimed. 'That isn't good news, surely. The last time we saw him he was deteriorating, slowly, admittedly, but deteriorating nevertheless.'

'True,' the consultant agreed with a twinkle in his eye, 'but this time he's back because a bone-marrow donor has been found. An urgent search has been going on because none of the family could be considered and we're now in a position to do a transplant.'

'That's great news!' Aaron enthused. 'At least the youngster is going to get a chance, and the sooner the better.'

'Tomorrow we will start the procedure, I think,' Charles Drury said. 'The donor is immediately available and once we've aspirated the bone marrow from him, the transplant can take place. Jack's parents are with him now and will stay with him until it's over. Then he will be in isolation. As we all know, infection can be a major problem during the recovery process after a bone-marrow transplant.'

When he'd gone on his way Annabel and Aaron went into the ward to see the boy. His parents were by his bedside and his mother said tearfully, 'What are the chances? How much can we hope?'

'We honestly don't know,' Aaron told her. 'Hope by all means. That is all I can suggest.'

She nodded, knowing in her heart that what the doctors were planning to do was a gamble, which if it was successful would give her son a chance of a normal life. If it wasn't, it would mean that what they had already faced up to would continue. As her husband took her hand in his there was hope *and* uncertainty in both their minds.

\*    \*    \*

'Could I ask you to come with me to choose a wedding outfit, Annabel?' Mary asked the next evening when she was having dinner with them. The ring had been duly admired, though the older woman had said in surprise, 'I thought that pearls were supposed to bring tears. I hope I'm mistaken.'

It had been a perfect opportunity to put Aaron's mother straight about a few things, but she'd merely smiled and said, 'It was the one I liked the most. Surely that's just superstition?'

And now Mary was turning the screw by asking her to help her choose a wedding outfit.

'I've bought a few new things recently but I don't feel that any of them are suitable for such an occasion,' she said, and Annabel could hardly refuse.

'Yes, of course, I'll go with you,' she told her with the familiar guilt surfacing. 'What did you have in mind?'

'Well, my friend, Alice, who is to be my matron of honour, is wearing beige, and I thought perhaps a long dress in pale turquoise or blue for myself. Tom and Aaron, who will be giving me away, will be in grey toppers and tails.'

'And I'm going to be scattering rose petals in a beautiful pink dress,' Lucy chimed in. 'What are you going to wear, Annabel?'

'I haven't decided yet,' she told her, thinking that sackcloth and ashes would be a fitting ensemble under the circumstances.

She had the cream wool suit that she'd worn over Christmas, or maybe she might wear a pale green dress and jacket that she'd bought recently. But what did it matter what *she* wore, for heaven's sake? She would be tense as a coiled spring, wondering what was going to

happen after they'd waved off the bride and groom.
Would she be the next one to be waved off?

In spite of her inward misgivings, Annabel enjoyed her
outing with Mary as she watched her try on various out-
fits and gave her opinion for or against.

In the end Aaron's mother found exactly what she'd
had in mind—a long dress of pale turquoise silk with
matching hat, handbag and shoes.

As her purchases were being wrapped she said, 'Shall
we celebrate a successful morning's shopping with
lunch?'

Annabel smiled her agreement, her mood still upbeat.
Until her companion suggested suddenly, 'Why don't we
look for a bridal gown for you while we're here,
Annabel? I can picture you in ivory or cream with your
brown hair and hazel eyes. Aaron tells me that your wedding won't be long once mine is over. I'm sure you
would appreciate having another woman with you when
you make your choice, and I mightn't be around nearer
the time.'

So Aaron had told his mother they would be getting
married soon! He had some cheek, she thought furiously
as the brightness of the day dimmed. What sort of a
game was he playing? The arrogance of the man! But
Mary was observing her expectantly and she couldn't
blight the other woman's happiness at this stage.

Yet there was no way she was going through the mo-
tions of choosing a wedding dress that she might never
wear so she said, 'I feel that I'd rather come another
time when I'm geared up for the occasion. Hopefully
you might be available then. If you're not, I'll ask someone from Barnaby's.'

Which just went to show how low she was on friends

and would be even lower when the woman making the suggestion was happily married and she, Annabel, had served her purpose.

'You do love Aaron, don't you, Annabel?' his mother questioned as they waited to be served in a restaurant nearby.

It was one question she could answer truthfully. 'Yes. I do,' she said. 'I think I've loved him since that very first day when he came rushing to the hospital to be with Lucy. I thought he was one of the most attractive men I'd ever seen.' She smiled. 'And the most bossy.'

Mary laughed. 'That's my boy. He does like to have his fingers on the pulse. Can't do with anything going on that he doesn't know about.'

'Yes. I *do* know that,' she replied.

'Of course you do, but that's all in the past, isn't it?'

'Yes. It is.'

If only it were true. His castigation of her *was* in the past, but it was spilling over into the present and casting a shadow over the future. But the woman seated opposite was not to be made aware of that.

Reverting back to her original question as to whether she really was in love with Aaron, Mary said 'The reason I ask if you love my son is because all the affection seems to be on his side. Sometimes I feel that you're cold towards him.'

And not without cause, Annabel thought grimly. Maybe she wasn't as good an actor as he. If she didn't know better, she would be tempted to think that Aaron was still as much in love with her as she was with him.

'Maybe I'm not as demonstrative as he is,' she said easily, as if what they were discussing was general chit-chat, and the subject was dropped.

She hoped she'd convinced his mother. Aaron would be upset if the pretence they were involved in fell apart. She would have to get her act together, play the part of the loving fiancée more convincingly.

When she stopped off at the house before going back to her flat he was there, and his eyes widened when she went up to him and kissed him lingeringly as if they'd been apart for ever, instead of having worked together until she'd left in the late morning to go shopping with Mary.

'What was all that about?' he asked when he went to the door with her as she was leaving.

She laughed. The sparkle was back in her eyes and his heartbeat quickened. But it slowed down again when she told him wickedly, 'Your mother thinks I'm not affectionate enough. I suspect that she's concerned that you may be marrying a cold woman.'

'Really? Well, do feel free to carry on reassuring her,' he said coolly, and she knew that he wasn't pleased for some reason.

As it drew nearer to the date for the wedding the feeling of unreality that had been there since the night Aaron had asked her to pretend they were engaged was increasing.

It was like being on a roller-coaster, unable to get off in the face of Lucy's excitement, his mother's happiness and his implacable purpose. She did manage to put the reason for it to the back of her mind sometimes and allow herself to enjoy being a part of the family again in the role of the other happy bride-to-be, because the tenderness and desire that Aaron surrounded her with came so naturally.

But every time she looked at the satin-like perfection

of the pearl on her finger she was brought back to earth. If life with Aaron was at present all kisses and cuddles, the memory of the choosing of the ring was a bleak reminder that all was not as it seemed.

The Sullivans' marriage was still hanging by a thread, with the erring husband performing his duties at Barnaby's with a sort of shamefaced bravado, and the wife tearfully seeking sympathy from anyone willing to lend a sympathetic ear. That person being mostly Aaron, who was still being supportive to Magda and the children.

So much so that Annabel wondered if his concern was activated in part by *her* misdoings. Magda seemed to be seeking him out at all times of day and night, and she thought it unwise of him to let the woman lean on him so much. If she had to open her heart to anyone, it should be her husband. Only that way would they reach some kind of understanding.

Sobbing in the arms of his boss all the time wasn't going to achieve anything, and how many deceived wives turned to the husband's friend or colleague as a replacement?

She was irritated and knew it, yet Aaron was the last person to get involved in that kind of set-up. He would be lowering himself to her own level if he did that. Yet she felt that he *was* overdoing the caring friend role.

When she went into his office one day unannounced because she thought the place was empty, Annabel found him with Magda nestling in his arms and he was stroking her hair.

He wasn't looking too happy and when he saw her expression his discomfort increased.

'Oops! Sorry,' she said, and glanced at her watch. 'I was expecting you would be at your clinic at this time.'

'I would have been,' he said stiffly, 'but Magda had a problem that she needed my help with.'

'Yes, I'm sure she did,' Annabel retorted smoothly, 'and so do all the children that are waiting to see you.'

And if that didn't earn her a telling-off she would be very surprised she thought as she strolled out of the office.

What she'd said had been a bit unfair because Aaron wasn't the only one seeing patients in the clinic. There would be at least two junior doctors handling the cases with him. But he was the spearhead, the one they turned to if they weren't sure, and here he was comforting that woman again.

He must have sent Magda quickly on her way as he caught Annabel up before she'd got to the ward, and she wasn't wrong about the telling-off.

'You just interrupted a private conversation in a rude and disruptive manner,' he said coldly. 'Who do you think you are? Accusing me of neglecting my patients.'

'Was I wrong?' she asked smoothly.

'Yes, you damned well were. Charles is taking my clinic this morning. Magda had asked to see me and he offered to stand in for me until I'd got her sorted.'

'I'm sorry. I wasn't aware that you'd made other arrangements,' she said, still unrepentant. 'But can I tell you something?'

'Go ahead.'

'You will never have that woman "sorted". It's time she stood on her own two feet like the rest of us have to do. If this is what she's like all the time, maybe there was a reason Terry looked elsewhere.'

'But, of course, you'd know all about that, wouldn't you?' he said silkily. 'It stands to reason that you'll see what happened to the Sullivans from the girlfriend's point of view.'

'I might have known you would think that,' she flared back at him. 'Well, Mr Holier Than Thou, just take care that *you* don't fall off your pedestal, too. That woman wants you. Say the word and her tears will be dried in a flash.'

'You're demeaning Magda's grief,' he said stonily, 'and ought to be ashamed. I suppose that somewhere in your moral confusion you see a justification for it, but don't start bringing me into it. All I'm doing is trying to help.'

'Yes, well, I hope that Terry sees it that way. It's a wonder he hasn't told you to mind your own business. And just for the record, though I don't expect you to believe me, I didn't know my American lover was married. He was plausible and charming and, like a fool, it never occurred to me to look any further. So you can book me down as guilty on that count, but not for anything else. And next time you feel like snuggling up to me in front of your mother, forget it!'

When she'd gone striding off Aaron stood staring into space as his annoyance evaporated. Magda *was* becoming a drain on him, but he felt so sorry for her and the children he'd had to offer support.

Annabel's outburst had come as a surprise. Surely she wasn't jealous. He shook his head. It was more likely her thinking he was making a fool of himself that had brought forth the floodtide of annoyance.

Knowing her as he did, he could believe that she hadn't been aware that the guy she'd had an affair with had been married. If he'd been as supportive to her in her sadness as he was being to Magda, he might have something to be proud of. But instead he'd condemned her without letting her get a word in edgeways and was now trying to make up for it with a sham engagement.

He felt suddenly weary. He didn't seem to be getting anything right these days. He couldn't see Annabel falling into his arms once his mother was married and agreeing to turn the pretence into reality after what had just gone on between them.

But there was no backing out at the moment. His mother was a determined woman. If she knew she was being deceived she would call the wedding off, and if that happened he would be devastated. At least one of them deserved some happiness.

So much for death wish two Annabel thought as she scrubbed up for a routine tonsillectomy some minutes later. She'd told Aaron to keep away from her and had pretended she'd meant it, when all the time she ached for everything to be right between them.

Her criticism of his behaviour had been out of order. If Magda *was* taking advantage of his kindness, his actions were innocent enough. And yet *she'd* acted like a jealous wife herself during their slanging match in the corridor. Was nothing ever going to go right between them? And did Aaron believe what she'd said about not knowing Randy had been married?

She was due to go round that evening to help Mary arrange the seating plan for the reception, but now wasn't sure what to do. However, her mind was made up for her when, answering a ring on the doorbell, she found Aaron outside.

'I was passing and knowing that you're due at our place thought you might like a lift,' he said flatly.

'Er…yes…thanks,' she managed. 'I'll get my coat.'

Reaching up into the hall cupboard, she paused. 'But it will mean you having to bring me back.'

'So what?' he said in the same monotone. 'I don't mind. After all, you're doing Mum a favour.'

Aaron was not his usual brisk self, she thought. He sounded weary, defeated almost. She wondered if it came from their earlier skirmish. Whether it did or not, an apology was due.

'I was totally out of order this morning,' she said as she faced him with the coat draped over her arm. 'I don't know what got into me. It wasn't my place to decide the depth of Magda Sullivan's distress, and I do know that you've been helping her from the best of motives.'

'Forget it,' he said. 'You were probably right. Maybe I have been too available for her. I don't know.' He gave a tired smile. 'Everyone isn't as self-sufficient as you and I, though at this moment I'm not sure if I've bitten off more than I can chew.'

'In what way?'

'Several. You and I being at the top of the list.'

'Am I supposed to understand what you mean by that?'

'Not really.'

'So explain.'

He frowned. 'I don't know if I can. I feel that I've given you a raw deal. Rebuking you like a Victorian father one moment and the next cajoling you into deceiving my mother.'

'Both things are understandable,' she told him gently. 'You do what you do because you love your mother and Lucy. You sent me packing because you thought I wouldn't be suitable for you or Lucy and the hoax we're playing on your mother is from the best of motives. With regard to *my* feelings on the matter, I may as well make them clear.

'I accept that I've been tested and found lacking with regard to us and Lucy. As far as your mother is concerned, I'm as anxious as you that she should be happy. But, Aaron, at the risk of telling you how to run your life, if I find that Lucy is going to be fobbed off onto childminders, you will marry me whether you like it or not. Because part of the blame will be mine.'

To her surprise he smiled. Why, she didn't know, after the ultimatum she'd just given him. Yet she'd meant every word. Lucy had been brought up without a mother, but she'd had a loving grandma in her life, and now she, too, was leaving her. Couldn't Aaron see what that was going to mean to the child? What had happened to his organising skills that she'd thought second to none?

'That's the first marriage proposal I've had in years,' he said, 'and knowing you, it would have to be different.'

'I'm not joking.'

He was serious now. 'I know you're not, and I'm sure that Lucy would appreciate your concern.' And he added with a smile, 'As for me, if the worst comes to the worst I suppose I'll have to marry you.'

'That's the deal,' she said, buttoning her coat before she locked the door behind them and telling herself as she did so that when it came to crazy conversations, the one they'd just had was in a class of its own.

While Annabel and Mary were discussing arrangements Aaron went into his study to do some paperwork that he'd brought home with him. When they'd finished what they had to do Annabel went to tell him that she was ready to go.

He was asleep with his head resting on his forearms on the desk top, and as she looked down on him she thought that she hadn't been wrong. He had been tired and had given in to fatigue. Aaron spent himself caring for others, sick children, Lucy, his mother and deceived wives. He gave little thought to himself.

She loved him unreservedly. He could give her the family life that she'd never had if only he would relent, but there was no way she was going to take the initiative. Aaron was the one who'd shattered her dream and he was the one who had to put it together again.

'He's asleep,' she told his mother when she went back into the sitting room. 'I'll get a taxi.'

Mary got to her feet. 'I'll take you home,' she offered, but Annabel shook her head.

'No. Lucy might wake up and Aaron is so sound asleep he won't hear her. I'll take a taxi.'

The next morning he sought her out before the day got under way.

'Why didn't you wake me up last night?' he asked. 'I said I would take you home.'

She smiled. 'It would have been cruel to disturb you. You were in a really deep sleep.'

'Not so deep that I didn't sense you'd gone.'

'How?'

He shrugged. 'I don't know, but I did. The room suddenly went cold.'

She laughed. 'That was when your mother opened the front door to let me out.'

'So that was it,' he said absently, and led the way to the two children's wards.

Three new patients had been admitted the previous day—a baby living in poor conditions had been admitted with hypothermia, a six-year-old with pneumonia and a little girl from Indonesia, recently arrived in England with suspected tuberculosis.

In the case of baby Alex a dramatic fall in body temperature had been picked up at the local clinic and the infant rushed to hospital where it had been given warm drinks, warm baths and had had its head covered to prevent any further rapid loss of body heat.

The bewildered parents, having no previous experience of hypothermia and being both very young, had been stunned to discover that their quiet baby had developed something that was life-threatening.

Alex's body temperature had risen almost immediately, but lack of warm clothing and heat in the home would have to be looked at before the little one was discharged back into the community.

His admission to Rainbow Ward had been followed by the transfer from A and E of the six-year-old with pneumonia who had been testing the ice on a frozen pond a couple of days previously and had come to grief when it had cracked. He'd been rescued almost immediately but had been taken home instead of to A and E and pond water in the lungs and the general effects of immersion had brought on pneumonia.

Of the three new admissions the child with the suspected tuberculosis was giving the most concern. She was being kept separate from the other children in a side ward while tests were being done. A chest X-ray had shown abnormalities of the lungs and the sputum was being examined for tuberculosis organisms.

She was coughing all the time and so far the large doses of drugs she was being given were having no effect. But both doctors knew that the bacteria would have been in the lungs for some time and a quick cure was not viable. It could take months of treatment before she showed any signs of recovery, but at least modern medicine did have a cure for most forms of tuberculosis.

At lunchtime Aaron sought Annabel out in the restaurant, and as she observed him questioningly he said, 'Can I ask a favour of you?'

'Er…yes.'

'My mother and Tom flew to Spain this morning on the spur of the moment to look at property there. They fancy a Spanish villa as well as the property they'll have here, and while they're away I intend to finish early each afternoon to pick Lucy up from school. But I've just been told that the clinical services manager for paediatric care has arranged a meeting here for heads of departments this afternoon and it's vital that I'm present. Could you possibly pick her up for me just this once? I've checked your list and see that you are free then and for the rest of the afternoon.'

She smiled. 'Yes, of course I will. Tell me where the school is and I'll be there.'

There would be just the two of them, she was thinking. She could pretend she was Lucy's mother for a couple of hours until Aaron came home…

# CHAPTER TEN

As ANNABEL stood amongst the group of mothers in the schoolyard, waiting to pick up their offspring, there was a lump in her throat.

Normally it would be her grandmother waiting for Lucy when she came out, and today it should have been Aaron, but due to circumstances he'd had to trust *her* with his daughter, and she wasn't going to put a foot wrong.

When the children came pouring out, Lucy was chatting to a friend and then she looked up, saw her in the crowd and her face lit up.

'Annabel,' she cried, and running across flung herself into her arms.

'I thought she was your mother, but you haven't got one, have you?' the other child said, observing them curiously, and Annabel saw Lucy's smile fade.

How many times had Aaron's daughter been faced with this sort of moment? Annabel wondered and, holding her close, she said softly, 'I'm here in place of Lucy's mum and I love her just as much.'

As the friend, suitably impressed, went to find her own mother Annabel saw that Lucy's smile was back, her confidence restored, and taking her hand they went to find the car.

They'd had milk and biscuits when they got in and played a couple of easy board games. Now Annabel was investigating the larder to see what she could make for an evening meal for when Aaron came home, when Lucy came into the kitchen and asked for some bread.

'It's for the robin,' she explained. 'There's one that hops around the garden and I feed it every afternoon when I come home from school.'

'All right,' Annabel agreed, 'but it will soon be dark. Don't move off the patio.'

She'd found some steaks and fresh vegetables and was setting the table when she heard Aaron's car pull up outside. Seconds later he came striding in, bringing a gust of cold air with him.

'Hello, there,' he said. 'Everything all right?'

She nodded. 'Yes. Fine.'

'Where's Lucy?'

'On the patio, feeding the robin.'

He nodded. 'It's getting very cold out there. I'll go and bring her in.'

He was back in seconds.

'Where did you say she was?'

'Er...on the patio. Why?'

'She's not there.'

'She has to be.'

'She's not.'

'Well, she must have wandered off into the garden, then, or come back inside while I wasn't looking,' Annabel said with calm reason, but when they went out together in the gathering dusk the garden was empty, and so was the rest of the house as they searched each room. There was no sign of Lucy.

Annabel could feel the blood draining from her face. Where was she? She hadn't been out there more than a couple of minutes when Aaron had come home. But the bread was there on the stone flags of the patio, and in her absence the robin was feeding itself.

'She'll be next door at Richard's,' Aaron said suddenly. 'The lights are on so he's home. She'll have wandered across. You can reach the coach house without going round the front of the houses.'

Even as he was speaking he was opening a wicket gate between the two gardens and striding towards the house next door.

As she watched him go Annabel felt the first sick stirrings of unease. Lucy had to be at Richard's, she told herself. Where else could she be? And with the asking of the question came the thought that there were a thousand places where she could be if someone had taken her.

But that was a ridiculous thought. It had to be. *She'd* been in charge of Lucy. No one else had been around. Nothing could have happened to her. She would be hiding somewhere, trying not to giggle as she watched them searching for her.

Aaron came back, his face grim. 'She's not there,' he said tightly, 'and Richard says he saw some guy hanging around the backs of the gardens when he came in earlier.'

'No!' she breathed.

'Yes!' he snapped. 'She might have been abducted. I'm going to ring the police.'

Annabel was reaching for her coat.

'Let Richard do that while we search the surrounding area. Every minute counts if she's wandered off.' Her voice broke. 'Or been enticed away.'

They arrived back in their cars simultaneously and each knew that the other had nothing to report. The police were outside the house, talking to Richard. Night had fallen and there was still no sign of Lucy.

Annabel was in a state of complete shock. She'd been only feet away while she'd cut up the vegetables. Yet it must seem to Aaron and the others that she hadn't been looking after her properly. He *must* be thinking those sort of thoughts and she wondered how long it would be before he voiced them.

All the squad cars in the area had been notified to be on the lookout for a fair-haired, five-year-old in school uniform and slippers. That was something else adding to the nightmare that had come out of the blue. It was a cold night and Lucy's winter coat was hung up in the hallway and her warm boots were near the kitchen door where she'd taken them off.

'I'm going out to search again,' Aaron said, adding when she got to her feet, 'You stay here, Annabel. Richard will come with me. We need someone here in case she comes back.'

His voice was flat, expressionless, but she knew that he wasn't like that inside. He was dying a thousand deaths—and so was she, especially as she'd been the one looking after Lucy.

Daylight had been fading when she'd gone to feed the bird, but they'd only been a few feet away from each other. The child must have disappeared when she'd gone into the larder for a second time. Secure in the knowledge that Lucy had been safe in her own back garden, she'd seen no danger.

But now it was starting to look as if there had been. That she hadn't been safe. She'd seen the parents of missing children on television, traumatised and fearful as they'd pleaded with those who'd taken their child to bring it back. Was that what Aaron was going to have to do soon?

They'd left a policewoman with her and Annabel felt

that, as well as being there for support, the WPC was watching her, debating whether she was involved in Lucy's disappearance. And could she blame her? She had been the last person to see the child before she'd disappeared.

When Aaron came back his face was like a taut white mask. A police sergeant and a couple of constables followed him in and the senior officer said, 'We're checking out what your neighbour saw just before your daughter disappeared. He reckons there was a man lurking at the back of the gardens. In the meantime, can you think of anyone who would wish you or her any harm?'

'No, of course not,' Aaron snapped. 'I'm a doctor, for heaven's sake, and when I'm not working I'm here with my family.'

'How long have you known Dr Swain?'

'A few months, but why? What has that got to do with it?'

'Just checking. We have to look at all eventualities. How did Dr Swain come to be with your daughter this afternoon?'

'I asked her to pick Lucy up from school. My mother usually goes to meet her, but she's away and I had an important meeting.'

'What is the relationship between the two of you?'

Aaron hesitated and when his glance met hers Annabel turned away. She didn't blame the police for asking questions. They had to know what the domestic set-up was as lots of crimes were committed by people the victims knew.

But this was unbearable. If Aaron didn't blame her already, the doubts that were growing in his mind would put her beyond the pale for ever. Yet it was an indisputable fact that she'd been alone with Lucy and she'd disappeared.

If only he would say something, she thought wretch-edly. Reassure her. Tell her that he understood. But he had more urgent things to think about than the salving of her conscience. His daughter had disappeared on a cold winter's night when only a stone's throw from the kitchen door.

The police were preparing to commence the search again.

'We'll be back shortly,' the sergeant told them, 'and in the meantime, if you think of anything at all that you haven't already mentioned, get in touch.'

When they'd gone Annabel said, 'I'm going home for a while. I know that Lucy's only been to the flat with you once, and won't know the address, but she does know that it's in the hospital grounds and might have found her way there for some reason.'

'You're clutching at straws,' he said tightly. 'Some-one has got Lucy. I know it.'

The WPC who'd been left behind was bringing in mugs of tea from the kitchen and she said tactfully, 'It's worth having a look at your place to be on the safe side. Children do the strangest things.'

'Not this one,' Aaron told her. 'For one thing Lucy doesn't like the dark. If she's alone out there, she'll be very frightened.'

And absolutely terrified if she's *not* alone, Annabel thought in silent anguish.

There were no signs of her at the flat. Annabel hadn't really expected there would be, yet she'd felt as if some-thing had been pulling her back there. Maybe it was because she was desperate to wipe out the nightmare with normality. To be near the hospital where she was always in control, instead of driving herself insane with the whys and wherefores of the terrible thing that had happened.

As she was locking up again the nurse who had the flat next door was just coming in off duty and she said, 'Hi, there. You're just the person I need to see.'

'Oh, yes?' Annabel said absently.

She had to get back to Aaron. She shouldn't have left him. Maybe there would be some news by the time she returned.

'There's a very agitated woman hanging about outside the hospital's main entrance, asking to speak to Dr Lewis,' the nurse said. 'I explained that he wasn't on duty at the moment but she was adamant that she has to see him.

'It's a good job the public don't know where you doctors live, or those who think they have a grievance or should have priority treatment would be forever on your doorsteps.'

'Did she say what it was about?' Annabel asked, putting her worries to one side for a moment. It was clear that the nurse hadn't heard the local news or she would have said something.

'No. Just that she had to see him before it was too late. Presumably she has a sick child.'

'Yes, maybe,' she agreed. 'I'm going to his place now. I'll stop by the hospital to see if she's still there. What does she look like?'

'Bright red fleece and grey trousers.'

The last thing Aaron needed was a distressed parent at that moment, she thought as she pulled up in front of the hospital shortly afterwards. The poor man was one himself. If anyone needed help, he did. But she might be able to point the woman in the right direction once she knew what the problem was.

She was huddled on a bench near the front entrance. Annabel saw her in the light of the car's headlamps and she was out of her seat and beside her before she had a chance to move.

'I'm Dr Lewis's fiancée and I'm a surgeon,' she said as the woman looked up with startled eyes. 'I believe you have a problem, and as he isn't available maybe I can help you.'

'It's him that needs help,' she said, raising herself upright. 'I heard the late night local news half an hour ago and they said that his daughter is missing.'

Annabel caught her breath. Had this been the reason she'd felt compelled to come back to the hospital area? she thought as she observed the dishevelled person in front of her. Or was the woman an attention-seeker? One of those members of the public who thrived on sensation? They saw plenty of them at Barnaby's.

'Do you know something about his daughter's disappearance?' she asked gently, knowing that she had to tread carefully.

'Yes. He's got her. My Roy. I know he has.'

'And why would that be?' Annabel asked in the same quiet voice.

'Because they took our baby off us this afternoon and Roy said that if we couldn't have our little Sally, Dr Lewis wasn't going to have his child.'

'So Roy is your husband?'

'Yes, an' he's the kindest, gentlest father. *He* never touched the baby. It was me. I couldn't hold her properly. There's something wrong with my arms and she keeps slipping out of them and getting knocked. But I couldn't tell anybody as I knew they'd think I wasn't a fit mother. Even Roy doesn't know I can't hold her properly.'

'And Dr Lewis, where does he come into all this?'

'The baby clinic where I take her saw the bruises and she was taken to hospital. He was the one who saw Sally and said she'd been abused 'cos she had bruises and two broken ribs.'

Desperate to know where Lucy was, Annabel forced herself to be patient. The woman was at breaking point. If she pushed her too far, she might clam up or even collapse, and that would do Lucy no good.

'He was beside himself when they took Sally,' she went on, this time without prompting. 'Got the car out, and as he was driving off he said, "We'll see how Dr Lewis likes having *his* kid taken from him."'

'What's your name?' Annabel asked.

'Janice. Janice Carter,' she said tearfully.

'Well, Janice, you're a brave woman and I'm a determined one. Where do you think Roy will have taken Dr Lewis's little girl?'

'They'll be somewhere around here.'

'What, at Barnaby's?' she exclaimed.

'Well, yes. He works here, you see. Roy looks after the boilers. He has a hidey-hole beneath the hospital where he goes to have a smoke.'

'And you think that's where they'll be?'

Janice nodded, but Annabel was thinking that they could be anywhere, the distraught father and Lucy.

'So why didn't you go straight there when you heard that Lucy was missing?'

'I'd have had to tell him it was me that hurt the baby and I was frightened of what he might do.'

Exactly, Annabel thought.

If the woman's husband was in such a state, what

might he do if the police surrounded the place where he was hiding? That was if his wife was right and he was somewhere in the labyrinth of passages beneath the hospital.

She would see for herself before she rang them. No point in raising Aaron's hopes if they weren't there, and every second was vital to Lucy's safety if the man was mentally unbalanced.

'Show me, Janice,' she said. 'Show me where you think he's taken Lucy.'

The boiler room was empty, as she'd expected it to be. If Roy Carter *had* taken Lucy down into the dungeon-like bowels of the hospital, he wasn't going to have her on view to anyone who might be around.

'Where now?' she asked.

'This way,' Janice croaked, and led the way along a dismal passage to where a heavy wooden door blocked the way.

'In there,' she whispered. 'That's where Roy goes for a smoke. See if it's locked.'

It was, and Annabel ushered Janice back to the other end of the passage.

'How big is your husband?' she asked.

'He's not small,' the other woman said. 'Six foot. Does a bit of weightlifting. But he's not violent. It's having Sally taken off us that's made him do this.'

Annabel nodded, not entirely convinced.

'We're going to go back there,' she said, 'and I want you to persuade your husband to open the door if he's in there. He'll maybe listen to you where he won't trust me. I'll stay out of sight until he's done what you ask and then I'm going in after Lucy. Do you understand?'

'Yes, I understand,' she said nervously, 'but what if he refuses to come out?'

'Tell him the truth. That you are responsible for the injuries to your baby and if he's a reasonable man he will see that Dr Lewis, and especially his daughter, have done you both no wrong.'

'None of this would have happened if I'd owned up in the first place, would it?' Janice said fearfully. 'Roy won't hurt me, but he'll never forgive me.'

'We'll sort something out regarding that.' Annabel told her reassuringly, 'but first we have to find out if he's in there.'

There was no answer the first time Janice called his name, and Annabel groaned. She called again and again and at last came a surly response.

'What you doin' here, Janice? Go back home.'

'Open the door, please, Roy,' she begged. 'Just for a minute.'

'No. I'm stayin' here until they promise to give our little 'un back to us.'

'Ask him if he's got Lucy,' Annabel whispered.

'Have you got the doctor's little girl in there with you?'

'Yeah. I told you he was going to pay.'

'Is she all right?'

'Go away. I've told you. He's going to pay for what he's done to us.'

'Tell him,' Annabel urged. 'We've got to get Lucy out of there!'

Janice was crumpling. 'He'll throw me out after this.'

'You've still got to tell him,' she insisted. 'Two innocent children have suffered through this mix-up and it's got to be put right.'

'All right,' she said wearily. 'I'll do it.' Raising her

voice, she said, 'There's something I have to tell you,
Roy, and when you hear what I have to say you'll know
that Dr Lewis was right. Sally's injuries *were* caused in
the home but not by you. *I'm* to blame for what's happened. It was me that hurt Sally.'

'Oh, aye? An' you think I'm going to believe that?'

'It's true. I can't hold her properly. There's no
strength in my arms and every time my hold gives way
she gets hurt. I thought if I told anybody they'd say I
wasn't a fit mother.'

There was silence at the other side of the big studded
door. Then they heard bolts being drawn back and it
began to open slowly. Annabel waited until the man
who'd taken Lucy was framed there and then flung herself forward from where she'd been pressed up against
the wall of the passage.

Startled by her appearance, his arm came up and a
clenched fist struck her in the face. As her knees buckled
beneath her the last thing she saw was Lucy lying on an
old blanket in the corner.

She didn't hear running feet outside in the passage or
Aaron's voice calling both their names in horrified anguish. She'd caught her head on a metal cylinder as
she'd fallen and was unconscious.

'Lucy?' was the first word to pass Annabel's lips when
the mists began to clear.

'I'm here, Annabel,' a subdued small voice said, and
as a little hand curled around hers a single tear rolled
down Annabel's swollen cheek.

'Thank God!' she breathed weakly. 'You're safe.'

'She's tired and bewildered but unhurt, thanks to you,'
Aaron's voice said raggedly from nearby. 'You're the
one who is causing concern, Annabel. You took a blow

to the face and as you fell you cracked your head on one of the metal cylinders that are stored in that room.'

'Where am I?'

'You're in an A and E at the Infirmary and are due to go for X-rays and a scan. Needless to say, I'm coming with you. Mum and Tom are on their way from the airport. They'll take Lucy home.'

'So he didn't hurt her?'

'No. The guy was just trying to make a point in the worst possible way. I've checked her over and she's not been harmed. When he found her in the garden, Carter told her that he knew where there were lots of robins and, forgetting all she'd been told about not talking to strangers, she went with him. When we found her she was patiently waiting for them to appear.

'As for the rest of it, I imagine that you know more than I do. But it can wait. You've been hurt because of us, Annabel, and I can't bear the thought of it. I should have been the one getting punched by Carter, not you.'

'I owed it to you,' she said painfully. 'I let Lucy be taken. It was up to me to find her. And if my looks have suffered in the process I won't complain.'

He bent over and stroked her swollen temple with a feather-light touch.

'It's what's happened inside here that I'm concerned about. You were out cold for quite some time. Can you see all right?'

'Mmm. I think so. But my head feels twice its size.'

'At this moment it is,' he told her gently.

The door swung back at that moment and a nurse came into view, followed by a porter with a stretcher trolley.

'The consultant will see Dr Swain as soon as the re-sults of the X-rays are available,' she said, and Aaron thought grimly that they were well and truly on the other side of the fence this time.

'We've done an X-ray and a CT scan and they show that there is bleeding between the dura mater and the arachnoid layers from a torn vein. We need to operate,' the consultant in A and E informed them some time later.

'That should be my line,' Annabel said weakly.

'Not this time,' he told her with a sympathetic smile, and Aaron turned away.

One nightmare had ended and another was beginning, he thought. If anything happened to Annabel without him having told her that she was the light in his gloom, the one he'd been waiting for all this time, he would go crazy. But the doctor was saying, 'The nurses are waiting to give you your pre-med and then we'll take you to Theatre.' He smiled. 'But I don't need to tell *you* the routine, do I?'

She shook her head and closed her eyes, and as Aaron's glance met that of the other man's he said, 'No time to waste, Aaron. We need to get Dr Swain sorted.'

He held her hand all the way to Theatre and in the moment of parting said softly, for her ears only, 'I love you, Annabel. Don't leave me. I'm sorry I ever doubted you.'

She was already slipping into oblivion so he didn't know if she'd heard. He just prayed that she had.

It was a Sunday afternoon a week later, and Aaron had gone to bring Annabel home from the hospital. The surgery had been successful. The clotting blood had been drained away through holes drilled into her skull and the damaged blood vessel repaired. And now, looking somewhat peculiar with half of her head shaved and the assorted colours of fading bruises still evident, she was about to be discharged.

Once she was over the operation and feeling less frail, she'd begun to question Aaron about the Carters. She felt sorry for them both, even though Roy Carter had been to blame for a night of horror and her ending up in hospital.

Janice had been very foolish not to tell him that she couldn't hold the baby properly, and knowing the long hours that he worked in the boiler room he wouldn't always have been on hand to witness her difficulties. He had hotly denied any harm coming to the child from himself and Janice, and when she'd been taken from them he'd flipped.

Knowing who Aaron was from working at the hospital and having no trouble in finding where he lived, Roy had seen him as the villain of the piece when actually he had only been doing his job and had been right in saying that the child's injuries had not been accidental.

Their little one had been returned to them at Aaron's and Annabel's request, and Janice's mother had moved in with them for the time being while her daughter was having tests for multiple sclerosis. A daunting thought, but to the relieved Janice a justification for what had gone before. Roy had forgiven her and now it remained for the two doctors to decide if they wanted to press charges.

'What do you think?' he'd asked one evening when he'd gone to visit her. 'Carter has much to answer for. I know he didn't hurt Lucy, but he hurt you, Annabel, and gave me some of the worst hours of my life. Do we prosecute?'

She'd shaken her head. 'Not as far as I'm concerned. That poor woman had brought it all upon them through fear that she would be found an unfit mother, and the irony of it is that is exactly what happened. She triggered off a set of circumstances that sent her husband over the edge, turned your life into a nightmare, put Lucy at risk…'

'And you nearly got yourself killed,' he'd pointed out grimly. 'I think the police will take him to court even if we don't.'

'Well, if that happens we'll have to plead for him.'

'I don't believe what you're saying,' he'd exclaimed, 'but if that's what you want, that's how it's going to be. You know that the WPC who was at my place had you down as prime suspect. She encouraged you to go back to the flat to see if Lucy was there because she thought you were meeting an accomplice. I told her she was crazy but she still rang the sergeant and that's why we were all there at the moment of truth. I'll bet she saw promotion on the horizon when she saw you with Janice Carter outside the hospital, deep in conversation on that bench.'

'Maybe it was as well that she did suspect me,' she'd said laughingly, 'as after what Roy did to me I would have been in no fit state to fetch help.'

Serious again, she'd said, 'I can forgive him for what he did to me. Can you forgive me for letting him take Lucy away?'

He groaned.

'There is nothing to forgive. If my past behaviour has made you think I'm a person who bears grudges, I've only myself to blame. But did you really think that I thought what had happened was your fault?'

'Yes, because all the time we were searching for Lucy you never said anything. Never told me that you didn't blame me.'

He took her hand in his and squeezed it gently as he said, 'It never occurred to me. You were hardly likely to expect someone to be lurking in the garden, and as you said at the time Lucy had been only a few feet away from you.

'*She* wasn't entirely blameless, you know, ignoring all the times I've told her not to go with strangers. But as she's only five years old and couldn't resist the temptation of going to see a lot of robins, I haven't said too much to her. Carter would probably have snatched her if she *had* resisted and then she would have been terrified. As it was, she saw the whole thing merely as something different, and it was certainly that. But I don't think she'll do it again.'

It didn't make the incident any less horrendous but to know that Aaron didn't think her incapable of looking after Lucy was like a bright star in her sky.

Yet nothing else was said. There was no mention of the sham engagement and what was going to come after it. When he left she felt deflated because she was no nearer to knowing what was in his mind.

It was the following day when they said at the hospital that she could go home on Sunday. When she told Aaron he said immediately, 'You do know that you're coming to us, don't you? So that I can look after you? Mum has your room all ready and Lucy can't wait.'

She swallowed hard. He'd said that he wanted to look after her. What did Aaron mean by that? As a doctor? A friend? Or a lover? It wouldn't be *that*, she thought. There were still things not said between them.

And now Sunday was here and the hospital was slow at giving the word to go. The consultant was late on his rounds and as it would soon be dark Aaron was in a fever of impatience for some reason. But at last they were off, with Annabel wrapped in a warm shawl beside him.

It was wonderful to be in the outside world again, she thought. Or at least it would be if all things were equal between them. But Aaron had said nothing since the other night and today he was on edge.

Maybe he was regretting having to repay what he saw as his debt to her and so she kept silent, thinking that if she hadn't felt so weak and purposeless she would have insisted on going back to the flat.

When they reached the house he went round to her side of the car to help her out, and as he did so there was the noise of a light plane flying overhead. At the sound of its engine Aaron looked quickly upward. Following his gaze, she did the same. Her eyes widened as she read the string of words on a banner trailing behind it.

I LOVE YOU ANNABEL they said for all the world to see. WILL YOU MARRY ME?

As she turned slowly to face him he was watching her, waiting for her reaction, and she said in dawning wonder, 'So that is why you were in such a hurry to leave the hospital before it got dark. Someone wants to marry me, Aaron. Have you any idea who it could be?'

Taking her in his arms, he said softly, 'I might have. But come inside out of the cold first.'

The lounge was empty and with his arms still around her he took her into the room and closed the door.

'It's a man who loves you more than life itself,' he said softly as his hold tightened. 'Who wants to waken each morning with you there beside him. You *will* marry me, won't you, Annabel?'

'I have just one thing to say to that,' she told him, her mouth curving softly.

'And what is it?'

'What took you so long, Aaron? Of course I'll marry you.'

With a whoop of joy he lifted her high in his arms.

'Welcome home, my love,' he said, and she knew with a sweet and magical certainty that he meant it beyond any shadow of a doubt.

There was a tap on the door and when he opened it his mother and Lucy were outside in the hallway, Mary's glance questioning and hopeful and the small figure by her side dancing with excitement.

'Yes!' Aaron cried, drawing Lucy into their embrace. 'Annabel is going to marry me! What do you think about that?'

'Wonderful,' his mother said as she observed the glowing woman in his arms.

'Super,' said Lucy.

On the day after the plane had flown over with its incredible message Aaron told Annabel, 'Richard has a pilot's licence and when I asked him for a favour he was only too pleased to oblige. Now, after such a successful outcome, he's hinting that he expects to be best man at our wedding and I've told him that it goes without saying.'

'Of course,' she said happily. 'I don't mind who does what, just as long as you and I are the ones to be joined together.'

The words had a magical sound—joined together, for always. She hoped that somewhere Eloise and the man she'd given her life for might be smiling down on them when that day dawned.

* * *

She'd watched a radiant Mary walk down the aisle on Aaron's arm on a cool crisp morning, with Lucy close behind scattering rose petals, and had rejoiced to see the happiness of the older bride and groom as they'd left for a honeymoon in the Seychelles. And now her own big day had arrived.

The night before Aaron had said huskily, 'I can't believe that tomorrow you'll be mine.'

'I've been yours ever since the night you came rushing into the children's ward, desperate to be with Lucy after the operation,' she'd told him. 'I thought that you were the most attractive man I'd ever seen *and* the bossiest. I told your mother so.'

'And what did she say to that?' he'd asked laughingly.

'She said, "That's my boy."'

'And, of course, I lived up to my name, didn't I?' he'd said, suddenly grave. 'By preaching the gospel according to me, instead of taking you as I found you, honourable, caring and clever.'

'Shush,' she'd told him gently. 'No looking back, I should have told you the truth from the start.'

When he'd finished kissing her until she was breathless he'd said, 'I'm going to give you babies, Annabel. Brothers and sisters for Lucy, to make up for the one you lost.'

She'd nodded dreamily. 'Yes, please, but for the moment I have all that I want. You and Lucy, a family at last.'

The organ was playing the bridal march, and a pale sun was filtering through stained-glass windows as Annabel walked up the aisle. This time Mark was giving the bride away and an excited Lucy was doing the rose petals bit again.

For the man waiting at the altar, his lonely days were over. Life was beginning again. And the smiling, brown-haired bride, walking sedately to meet him in a cream silk gown that rustled as she walked, knew that with Aaron by her side the future was opening out into a walkway to happiness.

*Christmas is a time for miracles...*

# Christmas Deliveries

Caroline Anderson   Marion Lennox

Sarah Morgan

## On sale 3rd December 2004

*Available at most branches of WHSmith, Tesco, ASDA, Martins, Borders, Eason, Sainsbury's and all good paperback bookshops.*

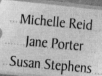

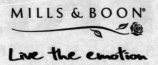

# 4 FREE

## BOOKS AND A SURPRISE GIFT!

We would like to take this opportunity to thank you for reading this Mills & Boon® book by offering you the chance to take FOUR more specially selected titles from the Medical Romance™ series absolutely FREE! We're also making this offer to introduce you to the benefits of the Reader Service™—

- ★ FREE home delivery
- ★ FREE gifts and competitions
- ★ FREE monthly Newsletter
- ★ Exclusive Reader Service offers
- ★ Books available before they're in the shops

Accepting these FREE books and gift places you under no obligation to buy, you may cancel at any time, even after receiving your free shipment. Simply complete your details below and return the entire page to the address below. You don't even need a stamp!

**YES!** Please send me 4 free Medical Romance books and a surprise gift. I understand that unless you hear from me, I will receive 6 superb new titles every month for just £2.69 each, postage and packing free. I am under no obligation to purchase any books and may cancel my subscription at any time. The free books and gift will be mine to keep in any case.

M4ZED

Ms/Mrs/Miss/Mr ........................................Initials ......................................
BLOCK CAPITALS PLEASE

Surname ...............................................................................................................

Address ...............................................................................................................

...............................................................................................................

........................................................Postcode..................................

### Send this whole page to:
### UK: FREEPOST CN81, Croydon, CR9 3WZ